KU-347-260

WITHDRAWN FROM STOCK

WITHDRAWN
FROM STOCK

'I want you to stay. Not just for the practice, but for me.'

There was tenderness in his eyes, but not just tenderness. She could see desire there, too. A hot and devastating and completely naked desire that made her heart kick up into her throat and her pulses begin to race. She wanted so much to reach out and touch his face, but she mustn't—because she couldn't give him a future, she couldn't give him children, and he was a man who deserved both.

Blindly she shook her head. 'Hugh, don't. Please don't.'

'Don't what?' he demanded. 'Don't say I'm attracted to you? Don't say that I want you? I can't not say it, Alex, because I do want you—you know I do.'

'Perhaps you think you want me right now,' she said, her voice trembling, 'but what you're actually feeling is pity.'

'Don't you *dare* suggest that,' he thundered. 'Yes, I feel pity for you, if you mean I wish to God you'd never had to go through the treatment for Hodgkin's alone, but pity sure as hell isn't the emotion I feel when I look at you.' He reached out and cradled her face in his hands. 'I want very much—if you'll let me—to make love to you.'

'Hugh... I... I...'

She couldn't say any more. Without warning, tears began to trickle down her cheeks.

Dear Reader

Can I make a confession? When I sent my first unsolicited manuscript to Mills & Boon I didn't know what double line spacing was, or the name of the editor of the line I was targeting. In fact—whisper this—I didn't actually know *what* line I was targeting.

Luckily for me, a far-sighted editor didn't condemn me to the farthest reaches of hell for my naivety. She might not have bought that first book, or the next one, but I learned something very important from those early rejections: that Mills & Boon editors are the most generous in the business, unstinting with their advice, support and help. And when I was eventually accepted I also discovered that becoming a Mills & Boon author means you instantly become a member of a global family. A family that not only brings out the brass bands for a celebration when things go wonderfully well, but is also just as quick to supply the hugs and handkerchiefs when things go wrong.

Love is the word most commonly associated with Mills & Boon® books. It's what the company was founded on a hundred years ago, and what I know the company will continue to build on in the next one hundred years. So Happy Birthday, Mills & Boon, and thank you for helping me to become the published author I always wanted to be!

Maggie Kingsley

A WIFE WORTH WAITING FOR

BY
MAGGIE KINGSLEY

MILLS & BOON®
Pure reading pleasure

All the characters in this book have no existence outside the imagination
of the author, and have no relation whatsoever to anyone bearing the
same name or names. They are not even distantly inspired by any
individual known or unknown to the author, and all the incidents are
pure invention.

All Rights Reserved including the right of reproduction in whole or
in part in any form. This edition is published by arrangement with
Harlequin Enterprises II BV/S.à.r.l. The text of this publication or
any part thereof may not be reproduced or transmitted in any form
or by any means, electronic or mechanical, including photocopying,
recording, storage in an information retrieval system, or otherwise,
without the written permission of the publisher.

® and TM are trademarks owned and used by the trademark owner
and/or its licensee. Trademarks marked with ® are registered with the
United Kingdom Patent Office and/or the Office for Harmonisation in
the Internal Market and in other countries.

First published in Great Britain 2007
Harlequin Mills & Boon Limited,
Eton House, 18-24 Paradise Road, Richmond, Surrey TW9 1SR

© Maggie Kingsley 2008

ISBN: 978 0 263 19879 9

Set in Times Roman 10½ on 12¼ pt
15-0208-53002

Printed and bound in Great Britain
by Antony Rowe Ltd, Chippenham, Wiltshire

Maggie Kingsley says she can't remember a time when she didn't want to be a writer, but she put her dream on hold and decided to 'be sensible' and become a teacher instead. Five years at the chalk face was enough to convince her she wasn't cut out for it, and she 'escaped' to work for a major charity. Unfortunately—or fortunately!—a back injury ended her career, and when she and her family moved to a remote cottage in the north of Scotland it was her family who nagged her into attempting to make her dream a reality. Combining a love of romantic fiction with a knowledge of medicine gleaned from the many professionals in her family, Maggie says she can't now imagine ever being able to have so much fun legally doing anything else!

Recent titles by the same author:

THE CONSULTANT'S ITALIAN KNIGHT
A CONSULTANT CLAIMS HIS BRIDE
THE GOOD FATHER
THE SURGEON'S MARRIAGE DEMAND

For Pam,
for giving me the key,
and showing me how to open the door

CHAPTER ONE

DR HUGH SCOTT stared with mounting incredulity at the plump, middle-aged woman sitting in front of him and decided his brain must have been well and truly out to lunch on the day, fourteen years ago, when he decided to become a GP.

I could have become a consultant, he thought as Sybil Gordon poured out her tale of woe. Better yet, I could have specialised in anaesthetics where the patients don't talk at all, but no. I had to decide to become a GP, and what have I got as my reward? The world's worst hypochondriac who is also quite clearly one sandwich short of a picnic.

'Mrs Gordon,' he exclaimed, cutting across her catalogue of symptoms without compunction. 'You cannot possibly have dengue fever. It's a disease that only occurs in subtropical areas, of which the north of Scotland is most definitely not one.'

'But my bones are definitely aching, Doctor,' she insisted. 'And I have a sore throat, and my nose is running.'

'Because you have a cold,' he declared, keeping control of his temper with difficulty. 'An ordinary, common-or-garden, September cold. Go home, and take an aspirin. Better still, go home and burn your copy of the *Family Guide to Health*.'

'But I'm sweating, Doctor,' Mrs Gordon insisted, clearly

not having taken in a single word he'd said, 'and I'm sure my eyes look yellow. Don't they look yellow to you?'

Heaven give me strength, Hugh thought as Sybil Gordon gazed anxiously at him. He'd been called out three times last night, had endured a long and wearisome surgery this morning, and this evening's surgery was turning out to be every bit as exhausting. He didn't need Sybil Gordon's hypochondria on top of everything else, and especially not when he had a new locum arriving at any minute. A locum he could quite happily have seen at the far side of the moon.

'No, your eyes do not look yellow, Mrs Gordon,' he said through gritted teeth. 'They are a perfectly normal, healthy, white.'

'Are you sure, Doctor?' Sybil Gordon insisted. 'When I stared at them in my bathroom mirror this afternoon I definitely thought they looked yellow, and my skin is starting to itch now, too, right here under my chin, which is another sign of dengue fever, isn't it?'

Heaven give me strength, Hugh prayed again, but heaven clearly wasn't listening because the temper he had been trying so hard to control ever since Sybil Gordon had sat down in his surgery finally erupted.

'Out, Mrs Gordon,' he said, striding across his consulting room and opening the door.

'I'm sorry?' she faltered.

'Not half as sorry as I am,' he exclaimed. 'Mrs Gordon, you do *not* have dengue fever. You do not have *any* kind of fever. All that is wrong with you is you're a woman with too little to do and too much time in which to do it.'

'But—'

'Do us both a favour,' he continued, his voice rising despite his best efforts to prevent it. 'Get yourself a job, or a hobby, because I swear...I *swear* if I see you in my surgery one more time with some ludicrous ailment gleaned from the pages of your medical book I will come round to your house and burn the damned book myself!'

He didn't give Sybil Gordon a chance to reply. He simply hustled her out of his room, catching a brief glimpse of his receptionist's shocked face as he did so, then slammed the door and walked angrily back to his desk.

Dengue fever. How in the world did Sybil Gordon imagine she could possibly have contracted dengue fever? Dear Lord, but the farthest the woman had ever travelled in her fifty-eight years had been the occasional visit to the neighbouring village. Built into the Kilbreckan bricks, Jenny used to say. The kind of woman who got homesick when she was more than a mile from her own front door.

A deep chuckle broke from him despite his anger. How Jenny would laugh when he told her. Except, of course, he thought with a sudden shaft of pain, Jenny wouldn't laugh because she couldn't do anything any more.

Hot tears filled his eyes and he had to bite down hard on his lip to prevent them from falling.

Two years. It had been two years since Jenny's car had hit that patch of ice and she'd skidded into the path of an oncoming lorry. Two years during which he'd thrown himself into his work, trying not to think, not to remember, but all it would take was something happening, something he'd want to share with her, and the realisation that he couldn't would make the pain of her loss as sharp and unbearable as the day it had happened.

'OK, you get to put this back up again when you can talk to our patients without chewing their heads off,' his partner in the practice, Malcolm MacIntyre, declared, pocketing the name tag from Hugh's consulting-room door as he walked in. 'Until then you stick to the paperwork.'

'I just lost my temper, OK?' Hugh flared. 'It's no big deal. I'll go round and apologise to her tomorrow.'

'Like you had to apologise to George Hunter last month, and Peggie Fraser the month before that.' Malcolm shook his head. 'Hugh, ever since Jenny died—'

'This has nothing to do with my wife.'

'You've been grinding yourself into the ground, trying to bury your grief in work,' Malcolm continued determinedly, 'and all that's happened is your temper's become more and more explosive. The people in Kilbreckan like you. They have done ever since you took over the practice ten years ago, but liking has its limits, and if you go on like this we're not going to have a practice any more.'

'You're saying I'm not up to the job,' Hugh exclaimed, and Malcolm let out a huff of impatience.

'I'm *saying* I'm worried about you. Hugh, Chrissie and I are your friends—probably your only friends since you've pushed everyone else away after Jenny died. You were best man at our wedding, you're godfather to our kids, and we… well…' Malcolm rubbed the back of his neck awkwardly. 'Dammit, we love you, you big lug, but you have to let go of the past, to move on, or Jenny's death is going to destroy you.'

Hugh's grey eyes grew cold. 'I'm never marrying again.'

'Who said anything about marrying?' Malcolm protested, pulling over a chair and sitting down. 'I'm talking about you needing to speak to someone—maybe seeing a counsellor, or talking to someone you can trust—getting your feelings out—'

'I have never done group hugs, Malcolm,' Hugh snapped, 'and I have no intention of starting now.'

'OK, forget the counsellor,' Malcolm said, 'but will you at least occasionally take some time out to smell the roses or, in our case, the heather? Dammit, Hugh, you're only thirty-nine—'

'We're too short-staffed for me to go traipsing about any heather,' Hugh interrupted irritably, and Malcolm nodded.

'Which is why we need another partner in the practice. I know—I know,' he continued, as Hugh's eyes rolled. 'It's my same old record but that doesn't make it any the less true.'

'Why do you think I agreed to us employing all these locums over the past eighteen months?' Hugh demanded. 'I know we need another doctor, but it's not my fault if none of the locums turned out to be good enough to be invited to join us full time.'

'Hugh, they could all have been a combination of Marie Curie and Albert Schweitzer and you would still have said they weren't good enough, because—bottom line—you don't want to replace Jenny. You think it would be disloyal to her memory if we did.'

'That's ridiculous.'

'Is it?' Malcolm leant forward in his seat and gazed at him searchingly. 'Hugh, nobody can—or will—replace Jenny. She was a special, unique person, but that doesn't mean no other doctor can—or should—take her place in the practice. We can't keep on working like this. You're exhausted, so am I, and when Chrissie agreed to become our receptionist three years ago she didn't expect to be working 24/7. Something's got to give, and it's already happening.'

Malcolm was right, Hugh knew he was, just as he also knew that if he wasn't careful he was going to lose everything he'd worked so hard to build in Kilbreckan, but how to explain to his best friend that he didn't know how to let go of the past, didn't know how to move on, didn't think that he could?

'Malcolm, I know I've been difficult to work with recently. OK—OK,' Hugh continued as his friend shook his head. 'I've been downright impossible, and I'm sorry. I'll try to do better, and I promise…' He took a deep breath. 'I promise if this Alec

Lorimer turns out to be even halfway decent we'll offer him a partnership at the end of his three-month contract. His references are excellent, you said?'

A faint tinge of colour darkened his partner's burly cheeks. 'Dr Lorimer's references are terrific—quite outstanding, in fact—but...' He came to a halt as Hugh's consulting-room door opened, and a plump, blonde-haired woman appeared. 'Chrissie, love, what can we do for you?'

'It's gone seven o'clock, and there's nobody left in the waiting room,' she replied. 'Do you want me to just lock up?'

'No sign of Alec Lorimer?' Hugh said and, when Chrissie shook her head, he frowned. 'Not exactly the best of starts when he was supposed to be here at six.'

'Hugh.'

'Sorry, Chrissie, sorry,' he replied, seeing the look she exchanged with her husband. 'Memo to self. Cut this new bloke some slack. Look, why don't the two of you get off home?' he continued, gathering up the folders of the patients he had seen that evening. 'Dr Lorimer won't expect the three of us to be here, waiting for him.'

Chrissie shot her husband another pointed look, and Malcolm coughed uncomfortably.

'Hugh, about Dr Lorimer...'

'Mr Sweetness and Light when I meet him, Malcolm, Mr Sweetness and Light,' Hugh said as he walked into the waiting room followed by Chrissie and Malcolm.

'It isn't that,' his partner began. 'Well, of course, I don't want you to jump all over Dr Lorimer's head on your first meeting, but...'

'But what?' Hugh demanded and Malcolm opened his mouth, then closed it again, and shook his head.

'Nothing,' he muttered. 'Nothing.'

It was clearly something, Hugh thought as Chrissie glared at her husband and Malcolm shrugged ruefully back. Maybe they'd had a row. Maybe they were worried about one of their kids. As godfather to their twins he should have known, but he hadn't seen either of the children in months. His fault. His decision.

'How are the kids, Chrissie?' he said awkwardly as he piled the folders he was carrying onto her reception desk. 'Still enjoying school?'

'Laurie is, but Tom wants to leave. He reckons they've taught him all they know.'

A small smile curved Hugh's lips. 'Perhaps they have. He's a pretty bright ten-year-old.'

Chrissie chuckled. 'He's not that bright. Look, why don't you come round to dinner one night soon? Tom and Laurie are always talking about you.'

'I'll do that.'

'When?' she demanded as her husband wandered over to the waiting-room window and stared out. 'You're always saying you'll come, but you never do.'

'I'll come soon, I promise,' Hugh replied evasively. 'I noticed Ellie Dickson didn't show up this evening to have her BP checked,' he continued, deliberately changing the subject.

'I've told her it's vital she has regular blood pressure tests now she's six months pregnant,' Chrissie replied, with a look that told Hugh she knew exactly what he was doing, 'but…'

'As usual it's gone in one ear and out the other.' Hugh nodded. 'I'll drop by her house tomorrow, remind her again.'

'Hey—Hugh,' Malcolm suddenly exclaimed. 'Come over here and take a look at this.'

'Unless somebody's handing out free money, I'm not interested,' Hugh replied, but he joined Malcolm at the window nevertheless and blinked when he saw what his partner was looking at.

It was a motorcycle, parked beside his Range Rover, but

not just any old motorcycle. It was a gleaming monster of red and chrome. A Ducati Sport 1000.

'Who in our neck of the woods owns a beauty like that?' Malcolm declared, envy plain in his voice, and Hugh shook his head.

'It can't be anyone local. If it was, the news would have spread like wildfire.'

'Not necessarily,' Chrissie said, peering round them. 'I mean, it's just a motorcycle, isn't it?'

Hugh and Malcolm looked at one another, then at her.

'Chrissie, that is not *just* a motorcycle,' Malcolm protested. 'That is a work of art. A perfection of engineering, poetry in motion, every serious biker's wet dream.'

'Boy's toy.' Chrissie sniffed, and her husband shot her a withering glance.

'A state-of-the-art mean machine, more like. I wonder if the owner would let me take it out on the road for a couple of hours?'

'No chance.' A muffled feminine voice chuckled, and both men turned to see a small and slender helmeted figure encased in black leathers standing in the waiting-room doorway. 'Nobody rides my baby but me.'

'And you are?' Hugh asked, his thoughts immediately going to their drugs cupboard though common sense told him no drug thief would drive such a distinctive motorcycle, or could possibly afford it.

The figure reached up and removed her helmet.

'I'm Alex,' she replied, holding out her hand. 'Alex Lorimer.'

Hugh automatically took her hand and, for a second, his gaze took in a pair of startlingly green eyes and a shock of very short and spiky red hair, then her words registered.

'But…you're a woman,' he said, dropping her hand as though it stung.

She grinned. 'Well, I was the last time I looked.'

'But your name…' He glanced across at Malcolm who seemed suddenly to be finding the posters on their notice-board extremely interesting. 'I was told it was Alec. Alec Lorimer.'

'*Alex*, not Alec,' the young woman said. 'Alex, short for Alexandra, but surely you saw that on my CV?'

He hadn't read her CV-couldn't be bothered to. He—*she*— had just been yet another in a long line of locums that Malcolm had hired as far as he was concerned, but Malcolm had read her CV. Malcolm would have known it was Alex, not Alec, and so, too, would Chrissie.

Malcolm and Chrissie, you've a lot of explaining to do, Hugh thought grimly as he watched his partner hurriedly introduce himself to the newcomer, and heard Chrissie practically chirrup a welcome while keeping one anxious eye on him, and the other on her husband.

'And you must be Dr Scott,' Alex Lorimer said, turning to him. 'The senior partner in the practice?'

'I used to think so,' he said tightly.

'Used to…?' the girl began, but he didn't give her time to finish.

Instead, he caught Malcolm by the elbow.

'I'd like a word in private, Dr MacIntyre,' he said.

'But I thought I might show Alex round the practice,' Malcolm began, then sighed as he caught Hugh's expression. 'Your consulting room?'

Hugh nodded, but the minute he'd ushered Malcolm through, and shut the door, he turned on his partner angrily.

'Just what the hell do you think you are playing at, Malcolm? You *knew* she was a woman. Every time I said his—*her*— name you never once corrected me, never once told me she was a woman.'

'Because I knew this was how you would react if I told you,' Malcolm threw back at him. 'So she's a woman, so what?'

'Because I *told* you male locums only, that's so what,' Hugh exclaimed. 'When you asked if we could have locums I agreed on the condition we would only have men. God dammit, Malcolm, you know what it's like round here. Our roads are appalling, the distances we have to travel are immense, and the crofters won't come anywhere near the surgery unless you bully them into it. How in God's name is a woman like that going to cope round here, far less bully anyone? She looks like a schoolgirl out on work experience.'

'She's thirty.'

'Then why is she still doing locum work?' Hugh demanded, quickly changing tack. 'She should be working full time in a practice at her age if she's any good. There's obviously something wrong with her.'

'There's nothing wrong with her,' his partner protested. 'You're over-reacting, getting this all out—'

'And where's she going to stay?' Hugh continued, talking over him. 'Have you thought about that?'

'In your flat, like all the other locums.'

'No,' Hugh exclaimed, his grey eyes flashing. 'No way is she staying in my flat. Can you imagine what the locals will say? Dr Scott's living with a woman—'

'No one will say that,' Malcolm interrupted with exasperation. 'Everyone knows your upstairs flat is completely self-contained.'

'She is not staying, Malcolm, and that's final. Phone up the agency and ask them to send somebody else.'

'There isn't anybody else,' his partner replied. 'It was Alex, or it was nobody.'

'Then we'll just have to wait until they can find somebody else.'

'You might be prepared to wait, but I'm not,' Malcolm exclaimed, his colour now as high as Hugh's. 'Look, let's cut out all this crap about her looking too young, and people talking if she stays in your flat, and her not being able to cope. You just don't want her because you can't stand the thought of another woman being in Jenny's consulting room, reminding you of her.'

'That's nonsense.'

'Is it?' Malcolm demanded. 'Hugh, we need her help. Even if we only keep her for her three-month contract, we need her help.'

'She is *not* staying, Malcolm.'

His partner stared at him for a long moment then his face set into grim lines.

'Fine. Send her back to the agency, but when you do you can also have my resignation.'

'Malcolm—'

'Either Alex stays, or Chrissie and I go, Hugh. Your choice, your call.'

His friend meant it, Hugh knew he did. It took a lot to rile Malcolm, but when he dug in his heels there was no moving him.

It's only for three months, Hugh's mind whispered. *You can surely put up with this woman for three months?*

But she doesn't even look like a doctor, he argued back. She's too small, too fragile, and look at her hair. Jenny's hair had been beautiful. Long, and thick, and corn-coloured. He'd loved running his fingers through it. Not that he could ever envisage a time when he might want to run his fingers through Alex Lorimer's hair, but what kind of woman would choose to go around looking like a pixie on crack cocaine?

'Hugh.' Malcolm's voice was gentle, pleading. 'Hugh, please.'

He wanted to say no, that no amount of blackmail would

change his mind, but he couldn't afford to lose Malcolm and it wasn't just because he was an excellent doctor. They'd been friends for over twenty years, and Malcolm had been with him in the good times, and the bad.

'OK, all right, you win,' he said grudgingly, 'but no way can she take that bike out on home visits. Apart from the safety angle, can you imagine what our patients would say if she roared up on it? Lady Soutar would have a fit.'

'She would, wouldn't she?' Malcolm chuckled, then his eyes sparkled. 'I don't suppose we could send Alex out on her bike just once to Lady Soutar? No. Right. Of course not,' he continued as Hugh frowned at him. 'I'll ask Neil at the garage to rent us one of his hire cars.'

'Make it something substantial, preferably a 4x4.'

'Will do. Shall I ask Alex to come through?' Malcolm added, and when Hugh nodded he hurried to the door, then paused. 'Look, I know she isn't what you wanted, but try not to judge her by your first impression. She might just turn out to be the answer to our prayers.'

Or the stuff of our worst nightmares, Hugh thought when Malcolm returned with Alex Lorimer and he couldn't help but wince at the sight of her short, spiky red hair.

'Who won, then?' she said as she sat down.

'Won?' he repeated, and a dimple creased one of her cheeks.

'I'm guessing the two of you have just had one almighty row about me so do I hang up my helmet or hit the road?'

'My conversation with Dr MacIntyre had absolutely nothing to do with you,' Hugh declared, and from the glint of laughter in her large green eyes knew she was not one bit deceived. 'I don't know how much the agency has told you about the practice,' he continued, deliberately changing the subject, 'but—'

'Just where it was, and that you wanted a locum for the next three months,' she interrupted. 'So which of you am I temporarily replacing?'

'Neither of us,' Hugh said, his mouth tightening. 'This was originally a three-handed practice, and we're filling in with locums until we can find the right doctor to join us permanently. I'll work out a rota for you tomorrow and Malcolm will take you down to our local garage where they should be able to fix you up with a car.'

'I don't need a car,' she replied. 'My bike can go anywhere. In fact, probably more places than a car can.'

'Be that as it may,' Hugh said, 'it hardly creates a good impression of the practice if our locum is seen racing around in leathers.'

'You're kidding, right?' she said, beginning to laugh, only to stop when he didn't join in. 'You're not kidding. Well, I'm sorry you disapprove of my bike—'

'Hugh doesn't disapprove of bikes,' Malcolm interrupted hurriedly, glancing uncomfortably from her to Hugh. 'In fact, we both had bikes when we were med students. Mine was an ancient Honda, and Hugh had a Harley, but the thing is—'

'You had a Harley?' Alex said, her head swivelling round to Hugh with interest. 'What kind?'

'A Sportster FXST,' he replied, 'but I don't think that's the—'

'Transmission?'

'Chrome 5-speed Harley,' Hugh declared, 'but we're wandering off the point here. Kilbreckan is a highly conservative Highland village, and the people in the outlying countryside are even more so. They will expect their doctor to turn up for home visits looking like a doctor.'

'Oh, for heaven's sake, I shouldn't think your patients would care if I rode up on a camel, dressed as a bunny girl, just so long as I knew what I was doing when I got there,' she protested. 'And whether you like it or not,' she continued as Hugh tried to interrupt, 'my bike has to stay because I can't drive a car.'

'Everyone can drive a car,' he declared, not bothering to hide his disbelief, and she straightened in her seat.

'Well, here's some stop press news for you, Dr Scott. I can't. I never learned, but if my leathers offend you I suppose I could always take them off when I arrive for a home visit. Unfortunately, as I normally just wear an all-in-one Lycra body suit underneath them, your patients might feel they were seeing rather more of me than they might like, but if that's what you want...'

Malcolm was staring at her in wide-eyed fascination, but Alex Lorimer wasn't looking at him. She was looking at Hugh and as his gaze met hers he could see the unmistakable light of challenge in them. Malcolm had been right. He'd warned him not to go by first impressions. Alex Lorimer might look as though a puff of wind would blow her away but she was also clearly a woman with attitude, and it was an attitude he didn't like. Not one bit.

'If you can't drive a car,' he said with an edge, 'then you'll have to use your bike, but can I urge you—'

'To keep my leathers on when I'm doing home visits?' she finished for him, her face perfectly bland, though her green eyes, he noticed, were dancing, and he gritted his teeth.

'I was going to urge you to be careful on our roads,' he declared. 'We don't have a lot of traffic, but we do have a lot of fools. It's also September which means it will soon be the start of the rutting season when the red deer come down from the hills, and if you hit one of them at speed there won't be much left of you, or your bike.'

She shook her head dismissively. 'I can take care of myself.'

Jenny had said that, he suddenly remembered with a jolt

of pain. They'd been having a row about her driving too fast, and she'd told him she knew what she was doing, that she could take of herself, and he should give it a rest. He had, and how he wished now that he hadn't.

Abruptly, he got to his feet.

'Malcolm, could you and Chrissie lock up, while I show Dr Lorimer where she'll be staying while she's working with us?'

Malcolm nodded, but when Hugh accompanied Alex Lorimer out of the surgery he couldn't help but notice that both Malcolm and his wife were standing at the waiting-room window, watching him.

Hell's bells, but what did they think he was going to do? Engineer an argument with their new locum so she'd flounce off back to where she'd come from? Dammit, he'd agreed to her staying. He'd even agreed to her using her bike. What more did Malcolm and Chrissie want from him?

For you to show Alex Lorimer some civility, his mind whispered. It's not her fault you've been blackmailed into having her. Not her fault she will never be able to cope here in a million years. At the very least she deserves some civility, and with an effort he cleared his throat.

'Did you come far today, Dr Lorimer?' he said, injecting as much pleasantness into his voice as he could.

'Just from Edinburgh,' she replied. 'I was spending a few days with my mother, then the agency phoned to say you needed me.'

Not you, he thought. We might need help but not from somebody like you, but he didn't say that.

'Quite a distance,' he said instead, and she shrugged.

'It took me just over four hours. I would have been faster but there were roadworks on the A9.'

'You must have put your foot down the whole way,' he observed, torn between being impressed and horrified at the sort of speed she must have been travelling.

'She is pretty fast,' Alex replied, patting her bike fondly, 'but then she has a 992cc, Marelli electronic fuel injection, V-twin engine.'

'Impressive,' he murmured.

She tilted her head slightly. 'The bike specs, or me apparently knowing something about an engine?'

'Both,' he admitted and, before he could stop himself, he added, 'How come you know so much about engines?'

'My dad owned a garage before he retired, and from when I was small I used to love watching the mechanics work, and it was always the bikes I wanted to ride, never the cars.'

'Which explains why you don't have a driving licence.'

She nodded. 'I got my first bike when I was seventeen, and by the time I was eighteen I could strip it down and put it back together again. My mother was horrified. She wanted me to wear pretty dresses, and go to parties, but I was only ever happy wearing a pair of dungarees, lying underneath a bike with a wrench in my hand.'

'A regular tomboy in other words,' he said and she gave him a hard stare.

'Just as well I'm not a rampant feminist, Dr Scott, or you'd be in deep trouble for that remark.'

Unwillingly, he felt the corners of his mouth twitch into a smile. She was quite a pretty young woman if you ignored her hair. Large green eyes fringed by unexpectedly dark eyelashes, porcelain-white skin that was so translucent he could see a small blue vein throbbing on her forehead, and a wide, soft mouth that was clearly meant for laughing. A water sprite, he thought as he stared down at her. Not a pixie, but a water sprite, and he wondered how her boyfriend—because she was bound to have a boyfriend—felt about her moving from job to job. He wouldn't have liked it. He would have wanted her with him. He...

Hell, and damnation, but what was he doing here? he wondered as he saw her lips begin to curve into an answering smile. He didn't need—or want—to know anything about this girl. She was just another locum. An annoying irritant who would be gone in three months, and that was exactly the way he wanted to keep it.

'I hope you've brought a lock with you for your bike,' he said coolly. 'Kilbreckan might look like a sleepy fishing village, but we get a lot of visitors during the season, tourists passing through, and your bike has temptation written all over it.'

'It's data tagged, and I lock it when I'm not riding it,' she replied as she pulled on her helmet, 'so if you or Dr MacIntyre should ever feel tempted, you won't get far.'

'Neither Dr MacIntyre, nor I, would dream of riding your bike without your permission,' he began defensively, only to bite off the rest of what he'd been about to say when he saw her green eyes were dancing again. 'Your flat's not far,' he continued, yanking open his car door with slightly more force than was strictly necessary. 'It's just on the outskirts of the village, but I'll lead, you follow.'

'I think I should just about be able to manage that,' she said, snapping her visor shut before he could answer, and he knew she was laughing at him.

Lippy, he thought grimly, as he put his car in gear and reversed. I've been landed with a lippy, spiky-haired water sprite, and if I wasn't tired…

You'd what? his mind mocked as he drove up Kilbreckan's High Street, past the harbour with its bobbing boats, then turned left at the corner shop, checking in his rear-view mirror to make sure Alex Lorimer was following him. Quit while you can, Hugh. Take this unsettling, irritating woman to the flat and leave her there because, right now, you're not winning.

Alex didn't think she was winning either as she followed Hugh Scott's Range Rover up the High Street.

'So much for the famous Highland hospitality,' she muttered to herself. 'So much for Highlanders always making a stranger feel at home. The man asked for a locum, he's got one, and yet you're obviously about as welcome as a return of the Black Death. Probably less so.'

Plus he was tall, too, she thought waspishly, which was another strike against him as far as she was concerned. Being only five feet nothing, she was acutely aware of her own lack of height, and she hated being looked down on, either literally or figuratively, and in the space of half an hour Hugh Scott had done both.

He's good-looking, though, her mind whispered, and unconsciously she shook her head. He might have thick black hair, a strong lean face, and a pair of quicksilver grey eyes, but he was arrogant and pompous and—

'Oh, for crying out loud!' she exclaimed, hitting her brakes as she saw Hugh Scott's own brake lights come on. 'What's wrong *now*?'

With a muttered oath, she pushed up her visor, and waited until Hugh Scott walked back to her.

'There's a problem?' she said, getting ready to deck him if he was about to make even the tiniest comment about her riding.

'We're here.'

She looked up at him, then at the imposing two-storied Victorian building they'd stopped beside, and her jaw dropped. 'This is where I'll be living?'

'In part of it,' he replied. 'When my wife and I bought this house five years ago it had been converted into two separate flats. We always intended turning it back into a family home, but…' His gaze shifted away from hers. 'We'll share the front door, and hallway, but your flat is completely self-contained, with three bedrooms, a sitting room, kitchen and bathroom.'

And it was as depressing as hell, Alex thought after he'd

showed her round. She'd stayed in some pretty basic places in her time, but somebody had normally put a vase of flowers on a table to try to brighten things up a bit, and there'd usually been some pictures on the walls even if those pictures were of distinctly manic-looking gambolling kittens, but this flat was functional in the extreme.

'It has a lovely view of the village,' he said as though he'd read her mind. 'And it's very easy to heat.'

So was a monk's cell, she thought, but she didn't say that.

'Right,' she said instead.

'Chrissie always gets in some groceries—meat and veg-etables and suchlike—for our locums,' he continued, 'so you won't need to rush down to the village shop on your first evening here.'

'Right,' she said again, wondering why it hadn't been his wife who had bought the groceries.

Maybe he didn't let his wife out. Maybe she was somewhere downstairs, having been cowed into submission after years of being married to him. Well, she had no intention of being cowed. Not by him, or by anybody, and something of her feelings must have shown on her face because he backed up a step.

'Any problems, I'm just downstairs, but as I said, there should be everything you need here—'

'So I don't have any excuse to bother you,' she finished for him.

A hint of betraying colour on his cheeks confirmed that she'd correctly read his mind and, as he made his escape, she was sorely tempted to yell after him that it would be a cold day in hell before she would ever bother him for anything, but she didn't.

Instead, she walked over to the sitting-room window and stared out. According to the agency, Kilbreckan had once been a thriving, bustling harbour. A place that had boasted more than a dozen shops where you could buy anything from a pin to a tractor but, with the advent of the car and new roads, it had become a village in decline.

It looked like one, too, Alex thought, but she didn't mind quiet places. She'd worked in city practices, town ones and rural ones, and she knew the score. In city and town practices you could be almost anonymous, but in a rural practice the patients would be disappointed if they hadn't found out everything about you within a week. Well, they were going to be disappointed, she thought wryly, because the inhabitants of Kilbreckan would find out only what she wanted to them to know.

She turned from the window and grimaced as her gaze fell again on the sitting room's bare walls and functional furniture. Homely it was not, but she was only going to be here for three months. She'd survive, and determinedly she unzipped her rucksack and took out a silver framed photograph. Once she'd put it down on the mantelpiece she was sure she would feel more at home, less lost, less…lonely.

'Oh, come on, Alex,' she said bracingly. 'It's not like you to get a bad attack of the blues.'

It wasn't. She'd trained herself to be always upbeat and positive, but tonight…Tonight was somehow different. Tonight, as she stared down at the photograph, at the familiar faces of her parents smiling back at her, and at herself, looking so young and optimistic, she found herself thinking of the man who had once been in the photograph. He was still there if you looked really hard. Just the edge of his jacket beside her father's shoulder, but he was still there.

'You're never going to go away completely, are you, Jonathan?' she murmured. 'Even if I cut out more of my dad, you'd still be there, just as you always will be.'

Sudden tears welled in her eyes, and with a muttered oath she put down the photograph.

Bloody Hugh Scott. It was all his fault, her feeling weepy like this. She hadn't expected a welcome buffet, a pipe band and a collective round of cheers, but she'd at least expected to feel wanted, and Hugh Scott had all but told her she wasn't.

Which was weird. He was the senior partner in the practice, so he must have agreed to her appointment, and yet…

'Maybe he's the strong silent type,' she said out loud, then shook her head. He had been anything but silent about her bike. 'OK,' she continued, regrouping. 'Maybe he's had a bad day. It happens. You've had them yourself.'

And maybe he's just an arrogant jerk, her mind whispered, and she bit her lip. She hoped he wasn't. It was going to be a very long three months if he was because no way was she going to run away from this job. Not only did she need the money for her future plans, she wasn't a quitter, never had been. She might have got off to a bad start with Hugh Scott, but bad starts could be rectified.

'Just be your normal, pleasant self, Alex,' she muttered as she went into the kitchen to investigate what Chrissie might have bought in the way of groceries. 'Just smile, and be pleasant, and everything will be just fine.'

CHAPTER TWO

A DEEP sigh broke from Alex as she gazed out of her consulting-room window at the grey-stoned houses of Kilbreckan, their slate roofs sparkling under the mid-September sunshine, and the harbour, empty this morning save for a rather rusty-looking trawler because the rest of the fishing fleet was out at sea. It was a beautiful spot, and the local people had been warm and welcoming, but after two weeks here it was only her pride and obstinacy that were keeping her from packing her bags and leaving.

A discreet cough caught her attention and she glanced over her shoulder to see Chrissie standing in the doorway, holding out a cup of coffee.

'Rough surgery?' the receptionist said, and Alex shrugged.

'It was fine. It's just…'

'Hugh.' Chrissie nodded as Alex took the coffee from her. 'Alex, I know he's being difficult—'

'Difficult isn't the word I would have used,' Alex said with feeling. 'Downright impossible would be closer to the mark. Chrissie, I know he's still grieving for his wife, and when you told me how she died…' Alex shook her head. 'He must have been devastated, but he has to let go, to move on. Taking his grief out on everyone because they're alive and his wife's not isn't good for him and it sure as heck isn't good for the practice.'

'I know, and the damnable thing is he's actually a lovely man,' Chrissie observed. 'There's nothing he wouldn't do for his patients, and he's a terrific friend. When he took over this practice ten years ago he could have asked anyone to join him but knowing how much Malcolm and I wanted out of Edinburgh, he asked Malcolm, but when it comes to Jenny…'

'He thinks every locum he employs is trying to take her place,' Alex finished for her. 'I don't want to take his wife's place, Chrissie. I'm here as a temporary help, and I'll be gone in two and a half months, and yet he can't even bear to call me Alex. It's Dr Lorimer this, and Dr Lorimer that…'

'You don't call him Hugh,' Chrissie pointed out, and Alex looked at her as though she was insane.

'Do you think I want my butt nailed to the wall?' she protested. 'He's made it plain he considers me a complete idiot despite the fact I've been a doctor for four years.'

'He doesn't.'

'He does,' Alex insisted. 'Take this morning. It's supposed to be his day off but is Hugh at home, with his feet up, eating chocolate biscuits and watching daytime television? No, he's here, supposedly doing paperwork which is Hugh-speak for keeping an eye on me.'

'It's…it's because you're new,' Chrissie said uncertainly. 'He doesn't know you.'

'And he's never likely to if he never talks to me,' Alex replied. 'If I so much as open my mouth at post-surgery meetings he gets this pained oh-my-God-the-village-idiot-wants-to-contribute expression, and I swear he must levitate out of his house every morning because I've never once seen him in the hallway.'

'Maybe he gets up earlier than you do.'

'And pigs might fly!' Alex exclaimed. 'Chrissie, he is avoiding me, and when he does meet me he behaves like such a jerk. How old is he? Thirty-nine. Thirty-nine going on sixty, more like, and a more pompous, arrogant twit I have yet to meet.'

'Post-surgery debriefing in my room in five minutes, Dr Lorimer.'

A deathly silence descended on Alex's consulting room as Hugh Scott's head disappeared from round her door, and her eyes flew to Chrissie's in dismay.

'Do you think he heard me?'

The receptionist rolled her eyes. 'Do you want the truth or a lie?'

'Oh, hell.' Alex groaned. 'He heard me.'

Which was just wonderful, Alex thought, reaching for her notebook as Chrissie hurried away. Post-surgery debriefing meetings with Hugh Scott were never a bundle of laughs and, after what he'd just overheard her say, this one promised to be a doozy. She should never have said what she had. She should at least have ensured her consulting-room door was firmly closed, but she hadn't, and now she was going to have to pay, and pay big time.

She did. By the time Malcolm had discussed all the patients he'd seen that morning, and every observation she'd made had been greeted by either a distinctly bored expression or an abrupt change in the conversation by Hugh Scott, Alex's pen had all but perforated her notebook and her temper was wire thin.

'Any problem with your patients, Alex?' Malcolm questioned with an encouraging smile that told her he, at least, was on her side.

'Rory Murray wasn't very happy when I told him he has osteoarthritis in his hip,' she replied, and Malcolm grinned.

'I bet he wasn't. Rory might be forty but he still considers himself the village Lothario, although Neil Allen at the garage would probably hotly dispute his claim. He'd think you were telling him he was over the hill.'

'He did.' She chuckled. 'But he cheered up a lot when I told him osteoarthritis can appear at any age, and it's actually been found in teenagers.'

'On what basis did you diagnose that he has osteoarthritis?' Hugh demanded.

Because I'm a doctor, God dammit, Alex thought, but she didn't say that.

'On the basis of a thorough examination, and my medical knowledge,' she said instead as evenly as she could. 'I have— of course—made him an appointment to have the hip X-rayed,' she added, fixing Hugh with her best *try finding fault with that* glare, 'but I don't expect my diagnosis to be wrong.'

'It's an odd condition,' Malcolm observed, glancing uncertainly from her to Hugh. 'You can examine a group of forty- to sixty-year-olds who have lived virtually identical lives, and yet some of them will have almost perfect joints, while others will have really quite severe osteoarthritis.'

'Hasn't research suggested that some people might have an inbuilt susceptibility to the condition, while others could actually have an inbuilt protection against it?' Alex said. 'I remember reading—'

'What did you tell Rory?' Hugh asked, cutting right across her, and she gritted her teeth.

Did he have to be *quite* so rude? Presumably he did, as it seemed to come so easily to him, and there was no need for it. Civility cost nothing but, in Hugh Scott's case, civility was clearly a completely alien concept.

'I told him he should try to keep as mobile as possible, taking painkillers like paracetamol only when necessary,' she replied, controlling her rising temper with difficulty. 'Obviously, if the pain becomes a lot worse, I think you'd be looking to prescribing anti-inflammatory drugs, and arranging for him to have physiotherapy, but at the moment I'd say it was a wait-and-see situation.'

'Absolutely.' Malcolm nodded, then the corners of his mouth lifted. 'Did he try to chat you up?'

Alex laughed. 'He did, actually. My diagnosis threw him temporarily off his stride but...'

'It didn't deter him for long.' Malcolm shook his head. 'You know, I doubt if even being told he was going to die would dampen Rory's libido. The minute he sees a pretty girl he automatically moves into wolf mode.'

Just as Hugh Scott automatically moved into disapproval mode, Alex thought, seeing his face set into rigid lines.

Oh, get a life, why don't you? she thought. So Rory Murray had tried to flirt with her—so what? As a female doctor, she'd very quickly learned that some men thought you were fair game but you fended off such men with a laugh, leaving no hard feelings on either side, and yet Hugh Scott was looking at her as though she was some sort of raving nymphomaniac.

'Did you recommend paracetamol to Rory?' Malcolm asked, breaking into her thoughts, and she nodded.

'I also suggested he try glucosamine tablets, and a cream based on chilli peppers,' she said. 'They're both available without prescription, and there's quite strong evidence that they could ease his discomfort.'

Was that a very derisive sniff she'd just heard from Hugh Scott? She *might* have been mistaken, but she didn't think she was, and slowly she turned in her seat to face him.

'Am I to take it you don't agree with my suggestion that he takes glucosamine and uses the chilli pepper cream?' she said with an edge.

Hugh leant back in his seat.

'I suppose it won't do any harm,' he said.

'It can also—in some cases—do a lot of good,' she replied.

'In some cases, yes.'

'Of which Rory Murray might be one.'

His gaze was locked on hers, and she thought, *Back off buddy. I've had more than enough of you over the past two weeks so if you know what's good for you, back off.*

He did. His eyes held hers for just a second more, then they slid away and he picked up his notebook.

'I noticed Donna Ferguson going into your consulting room.'

Of course you did, she thought, unclenching the fingers she hadn't even realised she was clenching. *You've all but got binoculars trained on my room so of course you saw her.*

'Apparently, she's not been feeling very well for the past six months,' she replied. 'Nothing specific. Just general fatigue, and feeling a bit stiff in the mornings. I noticed her fingers were swollen, but her blood pressure and heart rate were both normal.'

The supercilious look which made her long to slap him had disappeared from Hugh Scott's face, and in its place was concern.

'Both her mother and her sister died with breast cancer.'

'She told me.' Alex nodded. 'She's obviously scared witless she's got it, too, but I couldn't feel any lumps in her breasts or under her arms, or see any puckering of her nipples when I examined her. She took up the invitation to have a breast scan when the mobile unit was here two months ago, and her result was clear, so I think it unlikely anything would have flared up since then.'

'Unlikely, but not impossible.' A deep frown creased his forehead. 'Donna's mother died thirty years ago when she was forty and the treatment for breast cancer was nowhere near as good as it is now, but her younger sister died just four years ago at the age of forty-three, and she would have had a much better chance of survival if she'd come to us sooner.'

'I can see why you're worried,' Alex said gently, 'but I'm wondering whether she's just perhaps suffering from "empty nest" syndrome as both her daughters are away at college, plus her swollen fingers could simply be the first signs of arthritis.'

'Did you take a blood sample?'

Well, *duh*, and did he think that would never have occurred to her?

'Yes, I took a blood sample,' she replied as evenly as she could. 'It's in Chrissie's out-tray and will go off to the lab today.'

'I want to see Donna when she comes back in for the results.'

The words, *But she's my patient*, sprang to Alex's lips, and she crushed them down with difficulty. This case was clearly personal for him. She could see that, understand that, and if she also suspected he wanted to double-check her examination that was understandable, too. Just about.

'I'll tell Chrissie,' she said, and he almost—but not quite—smiled.

'Well, if there's nothing else…' Malcolm declared, getting to his feet, and Hugh stood up, too.

'There's just one thing,' Alex said, and the two men sat down again. 'I noticed you have a poster in the waiting room advertising slimming and exercise classes for women. As nobody turned up on the evening the classes were supposed to take place, can I assume the classes have folded?'

'Jenny used to run them,' Malcolm declared awkwardly. 'She'd weigh everyone who came in, give them a bit of a chat about healthy eating, then do some exercises. After she died I took the classes for a while, but as you can see…' He patted his ample stomach. 'I'm not really the best person to give dieting advice.'

'It's a pity the classes folded,' Alex said thoughtfully. 'Maybe they just need a new angle, something to kick-start them into life again.'

'You have an idea?' Malcolm said, and she smiled.

'Maybe. Let me think about it.'

'It hardly seems worth while restarting the slimming classes when you're only going to be with us for another two months, two weeks, and…' Hugh glanced at his watch '…three hours. They will only fold again once you've gone.'

'At least those women who are interested in losing weight will be able to get some advice from me during the next two months, two weeks, two hours, and…' she glanced deliberately at her own watch '…fifty-nine minutes, which must surely be a good thing.'

'I think it's a good thing,' Malcolm said hurriedly, but neither Alex nor Hugh were looking at him. Their eyes were fixed on each other.

'If you want to restart the classes, then feel free,' Hugh declared, indifference plain in his voice. 'But I don't want them interfering with the rest of your work.'

'Your wife couldn't have found they interfered with her work,' she said before she could stop herself, and Hugh's eyebrows snapped down.

'We are not discussing my wife.'

'No, we're not,' Alex replied. *Calm down, Alex, calm down. Oh, sod it,* she thought. *To hell with calming down.* 'We're discussing me, or rather your apparent inability to believe I'm capable of doing anything more challenging than taking someone's temperature.'

'Alex—Hugh,' Malcolm declared. 'I think you're both perhaps getting a little heat—'

'You wouldn't be here at all, Dr Lorimer, if that's what I believed,' Hugh exclaimed grimly. 'According to your CV you are adequately qualified—'

'I am *what*?'

'But I have to say I find your attitude less than satisfactory,'

Hugh continued as Alex gazed at him in outrage. 'Dr Lorimer, you are not here as a member of my practice, nor can I envisage a time when you would *ever* become a member of my practice. You are here simply as my locum, to do what I say, when I say it, and the only reply I expect from you when I say, "Jump," is "How high?" Now, Malcolm, about—'

'Just a minute,' Alex interrupted, her green eyes flashing fire. 'Just one cotton-picking, damn minute. I have not "jumped" since I was a junior doctor and some officious, overbearing consultant who thought he was God expected me to, and here's a news flash for you, Dr Scott. I will not "jump" for you. Not now. Not ever.'

'Alex, I don't think Hugh meant—'

'Oh, yes, he did,' she interrupted as Malcolm stared helplessly at her. 'That is *exactly* what he meant, and I've had enough of it. Enough of being patronised, being talked down to, and generally regarded as something the cat dragged in.' She bent down and retrieved her bag, her colour high, her breathing uneven. 'I am going out now on my morning visits, and when I come back I want a full and grovelling apology from Dr Scott or I'm walking.'

She slammed the door so hard on her way out that it actually rattled, and Hugh waited for Malcolm to say something but he didn't. His partner simply folded his arms across his chest, and stared silently at him.

'OK— Go on—say it,' Hugh declared at last.

'That you're an arrogant, insufferable son-of-a-bitch? I think that's pretty well self-evident, don't you?' Malcolm exclaimed. 'Get off her back, Hugh.'

'I'm not on her back.'

'Hell's teeth, you haven't been off it since the day she arrived,' Malcolm retorted. 'Alex is a good doctor, Hugh. Whether you like it or not, whether you like *her* or not, she's a good doctor.'

'If you say so.'

'Look, if you're truly worried about her professional capabilities, why don't you phone the agency, ask to speak to some of the doctors she's worked for?' Malcolm said, and when Hugh didn't meet his gaze he nodded slowly. 'You've already done that, haven't you?'

Hugh had and, without exception, all the GPs he'd talked to had been lavish in their praise.

'Excellent medical skills,' they'd said. 'A true original who really shakes your practice up.'

Nobody had wanted her to leave. All of them had wanted her to stay on, but she'd refused them all.

'It doesn't make sense, Malcolm,' he exclaimed. 'If she's as good as everyone says she is, why does she keep moving from post to post instead of accepting one of the partnerships she's been offered?'

'Itchy feet—good for the short term but easily bored?' Malcolm shook his head. 'It's not me you should be asking that question, but Alex.'

Hugh's lips thinned. 'We don't exactly talk.'

'I know, and you should.' Malcolm stood up. 'I like her, Hugh.'

'Well, good for you.'

Malcolm opened his mouth, then shook his head.

'I have to go. Sister Mackay will be expecting me at the old folks' home, and I'm already half an hour late, but you'd better get yourself a personality transplant, and fast, Hugh, or Alex won't be the only one who's walking.'

And Malcolm just didn't understand, Hugh thought, as he threw down his pen after his partner left. It was all very well for him to say Alex Lorimer was a good doctor, but he was hardly sitting in her consulting room, watching her.

All those other doctors wouldn't have said she was good,

if she wasn't, his mind argued back, and he let out a muttered exclamation.

Look at how she dressed for work. If she wasn't wearing jeans and a sweatshirt in the surgery, she was in her leathers when she was out on the road, and it was sloppy, unprofessional.

Thirty-nine going on sixty.

OK, all right. Maybe her clothes were unimportant, and he wasn't so much slipping into middle age as racing to embrace it, but she didn't take the profession seriously enough. All the laughter he kept hearing coming from her consulting room…

Thirty-nine going on sixty, Hugh.

OK, so maybe he was getting old before his time, but who the hell did she think she was, waltzing in here on her Ducati 1000, making everybody like her, arguing with him all the time? She was the one at fault, not him.

Except she wasn't, he thought, as he stared, unseeing, at his consulting-room wall. This had nothing to do with the way Alex dressed, or the laughter that always seemed to follow her around. It wasn't about her, it was about him. His grief and his inability to deal with it.

It was the pointlessness of Jenny's death that hurt the most. A small patch of ice on the road. A patch of ice that might not have been there if she'd been just that little bit later going out on her morning visits and the sun had come out. A small patch of ice he might have avoided if he'd taken the visits instead of her.

Why had she needed to die? Time and time again he had asked himself that question, and there was never an answer.

'Sorry to disturb you, Hugh,' Chrissie said, looking pale and tense as she opened his consulting-room door. 'Sgt Tulloch's just phoned to say a van's overturned on the A838. One casualty—Ewan Allen. Bill's closed the road, and he's called out the air ambulance and fire brigade.'

Hugh swore under his breath as he reached for their portable defibrillator, oxygen cylinder and trauma bag. If the police sergeant had called out the air ambulance then it wasn't good.

'Phone Malcolm at St Catherine's,' he said as he headed for the door. 'Tell him to meet me at the accident.'

Chrissie said something in reply, but he didn't catch what it was. All he was thinking, as he got into his car, was he'd bet a pound to a penny Ewan Allen had been speeding. The twenty-year-old seemed to regard himself as invincible, and on this occasion Hugh could only hope he was right.

He hoped it even more when he arrived at the scene and saw the crushed wreckage of Ewan's van wedged at a grotesque angle between two trees.

'From the skid marks on the road, I'd say he was driving too fast and had to break sharply to avoid hitting a deer,' Sgt Tulloch declared as Hugh carefully picked his way towards him through the broken glass and pieces of metal strewn across the road. 'The van seems to have somersaulted a couple of times before it smashed into those trees.'

'Nasty,' Hugh murmured, and the policeman nodded.

'It gets nastier, I'm afraid. The driver's door is wedged tight against one of the trees, the passenger door is completely crushed in, and part of the roof is bent. There's no way we're going to get him out of there without cutting equipment, and to even get to him you're going to have to climb into the van through the back doors.'

'I'll manage,' Hugh replied, but when he wriggled into the van to make his initial examination he very quickly realised that it was going to be downright impossible for him to do anything but secure a cervical collar around Ewan Allen's neck.

The only person who would be able to give the youngster any kind of meaningful medical attention was somebody a whole lot smaller than he was.

'Dr MacIntyre might have more luck,' Sgt Tulloch said when Hugh had eased himself back out of the van and explained his difficulty. 'He's a couple of inches shorter than you, isn't he?'

Yes, but Malcolm was also at least ten kilos heavier, Hugh thought grimly, but one of them was somehow going to have to get close enough to Ewan to treat him.

'Any word of when the air ambulance will get here?' he asked, and the policeman grimaced.

'We're not winning on that one either, Doc. Apparently there's thick fog in the central Highlands so they're coming up by the coast which means they can't give us an ETA.' The policeman turned as they both heard the sound of approaching vehicles. 'At least that sounds like the fire crew and Dr MacIntyre.'

It was certainly the fire crew, but it wasn't Malcolm.

'I know I'm the last person you want to see,' Alex said defensively as she got off her bike and walked towards him, 'but Chrissie called me because I was closer.' She sucked in her breath as she stared at Ewan Allen's van. 'Holy mackerel.'

'Too right,' Hugh said, brushing shards of broken glass from his jacket. 'We've one casualty. Ewan Allen, aged twenty.'

'Any relation to the Neil Allen that Malcolm was talking about earlier?' she asked.

'He's one of his brothers. There's eight Allen boys in all, ranging in age from six to thirty, and wherever they go trouble is sure to follow.'

'It looks as though Ewan met trouble head on this morning,' Alex observed, and Hugh nodded.

'It's even worse than it looks,' he said. 'He's wedged in tight in the van, and all I can see of him is his head and upper body. I've got a cervical collar round his neck, but he can't talk because he's so short of breath. I'm guessing he has a thoracic injury, which means he needs to be nasally intubated, but there's not enough space in the van for me to do it.'

'I'm a lot smaller than you are,' Alex pointed out. 'I could do it if you can squeeze in behind me, and pass me everything I need.'

It made sense, but that didn't mean Hugh had to like it, and Jock Sutherland, the head of the fire crew, liked it even less.

'I'd be a lot happier if you'd both wait until we drain the van's fuel tank,' he declared. 'It's clearly shot, and if this thing blows when you're both inside there using oxygen…'

'We'll meet our maker rather sooner than we would have wished,' Alex finished for him. 'But we can't wait. Ewan needs help now.'

The head of the fire crew looked at Hugh, and Hugh gazed indecisively back.

There had been nights after Jenny was killed when he'd longed to die. Nights when he'd never wanted to face another dawn, but he didn't want anything happening to Alex. She might be lippy and irritating, but she had her whole future ahead of her.

'Look, I know you don't think much of me,' Alex said, clearly misinterpreting his frown, 'but it's me or it's no one, isn't it? And the longer we wait, the less chance Ewan has of surviving this.'

'I wasn't wondering whether you *could* do it, but whether you *should*,' Hugh said quickly, and she threw him an *I don't believe you* look.

'Whatever,' she said. 'So, do I go in or not?'

It was dangerous, so very dangerous, but Hugh knew they had no other choice.

'OK,' he said, and Jock Sutherland shook his head.

'I think you're both insane, but it's your call, Docs. We'll start draining the fuel tank while you're in there, but for God's sake don't strike any matches.'

Or make any sudden movements, Hugh added for him mentally as Alex began inching her way into the van towards the driver's seat, and he followed, dragging the portable oxygen cylinder and trauma kit with him, and the van creaked ominously.

'Can you get close enough to him to nasally intubate him?' he asked as Alex half turned onto her back.

'It's tight, but I'll manage,' she replied. 'Ewan, my name's Alex—Alex Lorimer—and I'm a doctor,' she said as the young man suddenly moaned. 'No, don't try to turn your head,' she added quickly, as Ewan attempted to do just that. 'I'm going to put a tube up your nose to help you breathe. It will be a bit uncomfortable going in, but it will help, OK?'

Ewan nodded, and carefully Alex began to insert the tube up his nose, pushing it only when the young man took in a ragged breath.

'Is it in?' Hugh asked when Alex rolled back onto her stomach, and she nodded.

'Can you pass me an IV line?'

He did as she asked. 'Injury assessment?'

'His right arm looks to be fractured in a couple of places, and he's definitely got some unstable rib fractures. I can't get to his back, or the rest of him to check, but I'm guessing pretty major pelvic damage, plus probable damage to his legs.'

'BP, and respiratory rate?'

'BP 90 over 30, respiratory rate 40,' Alex replied, then glanced over her shoulder, her large green eyes contrite, as Hugh let out a muttered oath. 'I'm sorry—did I just kick you in the ribs?'

She had, but considering what he'd said to her this morning he was amazed she should feel the need to apologise. He doubted if he would have done and, as he stared back at her, he suddenly realised something else.

She didn't need to be here, risking her life for a young man she didn't know. OK, so she was a doctor, and had taken an oath never to turn her back on suffering, but she could have told Chrissie to get Malcolm. After two weeks of relentless needling from him, he wouldn't have blamed her if she had, but she'd come. Come even though he'd questioned her competence, come even though he had—as she'd so rightly pointed out—treated her like something the cat had dragged in.

It wasn't her fault she wasn't Jenny. It wasn't her fault she was very much alive and Jenny wasn't. He'd been determined right from the start not to see any good in her, only that her presence in Jenny's consulting room was an affront to his grief, a denial of Jenny's very existence, and he had been wrong, so very wrong.

'Dr Scott...?'

She was looking at him in confusion, and with embarrassment he realised she must have been waiting for him to answer.

'Forget about me,' he said brusquely. 'How's Ewan doing?'

'He's obviously in a lot of pain. I know the OR staff won't be happy, but I think we should give him morphine.'

'So do I,' Hugh replied, 'but titrate it in a little at a time.'

'Will do.' For a moment she worked on Ewan, then she glanced over her shoulder again and lowered her voice. 'Our portable oxygen tank isn't going to last very long. How soon do you think it will be before the air ambulance gets here?'

'I've no idea,' he muttered back. 'They're coming by the coast because of fog in the central Highlands, so it could be quick, or...'

She bit her lip. 'I hope it's quick.'

So did Hugh as the head of the fire crew called to him.

'I'll be back in a moment,' he told Alex.

'Take your time,' she said. 'I'm not going anywhere.'

'Spunky new locum you've got there,' Jock Sutherland declared when Hugh had clambered back out of the van.

She was. She was also a very good doctor. Hugh had been able to see her hands when she'd inserted the nasal intubation tube and the IV line, and the skill with which she'd dealt with both had been impressive. So, too, was the calm, matter-of-fact way she kept speaking to Ewan. If she was scared to death in that van—and she had every right to be-she wasn't showing any sign of it, and when Hugh thought of how unremittingly rude he'd been towards her since she'd arrived…

Unconsciously, he shook his head. Malcolm was right. He owed her an apology—a big one.

'We've drained the tank,' Jock Sutherland continued, 'and we're now going to cut and prise off the passenger side of the van. We'll be as careful as we can but I have to warn you, the van's going to shudder like crazy.'

It did.

'Maybe we should add ear plugs to our trauma kits,' Alex said, with a shaky laugh, as she wedged herself tighter against Ewan to try to keep him immobile as the van shook and groaned around them.

There was dirt and oil on her face, but underneath it Hugh could see she looked even paler than usual.

'Are you OK?' he asked.

She faked a smile. 'Just stiff from the way I'm lying.'

'You're sure?' he insisted. 'There's a lot of broken glass—'

'I'm fine,' she snapped, then shook her head as he blinked. 'Sorry. Mega-overreaction. I just…I don't like people fussing over me.'

She obviously didn't, but then he didn't much like it either, he thought, remembering the way Malcolm had tried to comfort him after Jenny's death, and how very rude he'd been in return.

'I'm sure it won't be much longer now,' he said encouragingly, and Alex smiled again, this time a real one.

'I'll hold you to that,' she said.

To Hugh's relief, it didn't take long for the fire crew to get the side off the van and the minute it was gone he clambered in. Carefully, he and Alex began easing Ewan's hips and torso out from under the demolished dashboard, keeping his back in as much of an alignment as possible, then Hugh swore.

'What's wrong?' Alex asked.

'He's not moving. I don't know why, but I can't shift him.'

The fire chief squinted round Hugh, and swore even more volubly.

'It's his foot, Doc. His foot's twisted right round the brake pedal, and it's stuck tight.'

Alex's gaze met Hugh's, and he knew what she was thinking. Unless they could loosen Ewan's foot they would have to amputate it because he couldn't stay in the van any longer. Already they could already see his injuries were far more extensive than Alex had previously thought. His pelvis was definitely fractured, but his abdomen was tense and distended, both of his femurs were broken, and his ankle had an open, angulated fracture.

'I…I suppose if it has to be done,' Alex said uncertainly, and Hugh reached down and felt Ewan's foot.

It was ice cold. It would probably have to be amputated in the hospital anyway, but he had to give Ewan this one chance. Had to.

'Jock, have you a set of the jaws of life?' he said, and the fire chief nodded and disappeared.

'What's the jaws of life?' Alex asked, clearly puzzled.

'It's a hydraulic tool that looks a bit like an enormous pair of scissors,' Hugh explained. 'With luck, Jock might be able to clamp the jaws round the top of the brake pedal, and if he pulls on the pedal, and I pull on Ewan's foot, we might be able to get him free.'

Alex nodded, but Jock Sutherland didn't when he came back and Hugh explained his idea.

'Hell, Doc, do you realise I could take off a couple of your fingers doing that?' he protested.

'Just do it, OK?' Hugh said, and the fire chief started to argue again, then took one look at Hugh's face and shrugged.

'Your fingers, Doc.'

Fingers he would most certainly need if he wanted to remain a doctor, Hugh realised as Jock stretched past him with the jaws of life, but there was no time for second thoughts. The fire chief hadn't suggested an alternative, so it was this or nothing.

'Ready, Jock?' he said, and when the fire chief nodded, Hugh took a deep breath, and shouted, 'Pull!'

For a minute both men strained their hardest, then Alex let out an ear-splitting whoop.

'It's out!' she exclaimed, her eyes very bright. 'You did it, Hugh. You did it!'

Dimly he was aware that she'd called him by his Christian name, and that Jock Sutherland was slapping him on the back, but what he was most aware of was the whir of helicopter blades overhead and he sent up a silent prayer of thanks.

Within minutes the air ambulance paramedics had transferred Ewan to a backboard, inserted fresh IV lines, and the helicopter had taken off again. Bill Tulloch set off to organise a clean-up of the road, and after many comments of, 'The pair of you must have charmed lives,' Jock and his fire crew finally left too.

'Do you think Ewan will make it?' Alex asked as she and Hugh walked over to her motorcycle.

'I hope so,' Hugh replied, then cleared his throat. 'Thanks for your help.'

'It's what I'm here for.' She met his gaze. 'At least it's supposed to be what I'm here for—to help—if you'll let me.'

'After witnessing what you just did, you bet I'll let you,' he replied. 'You did a great job.'

She blinked, then her expression changed to one of exaggerated disbelief.

'Did mine ears deceive me or did you actually—could you possibly—have just paid me a compliment?'

'Alex—'

'And you've just called me by my Christian name,' she exclaimed. 'Praise the lord, another first.'

He gave her a very hard stare. 'Are you always this much trouble wherever you work?'

'Oh, absolutely.' She nodded, and when his lips twitched into a reluctant smile, she added, 'I'm also a good doctor, Hugh, but I don't want to take Jenny's place. I'm here simply because your practice needs some help, and in two and a half months I'll be out of your hair, but in the meantime what say we call a truce?'

He thrust his fingers through his black hair awkwardly. 'That crack I made earlier—about jumping when I say jump—I'm sorry. I was out of line.'

'Yes, you were,' she said, 'but I was out of line, too, when I said you were a pompous, arrogant twit.'

'Actually, it was the "thirty-nine going on sixty" bit that hit home hardest,' he said ruefully.

'I'm sorry about that,' she said, looking as though she meant it. 'Look, what say we make a bargain? You forget what I said, and I'll forget what you said.'

'You're a lot more forgiving than I would be in your shoes,' he said, and she smiled.

'I'm not a bad person, Hugh.'

'Which makes me…?'

She tilted her head thoughtfully. 'I don't know. I haven't figured you out yet.' She glanced down at her watch and let out a muttered oath. 'I'd better go. I haven't even made my first home visit yet and it's almost half past one.'

'Wait a minute,' he said as she reached for her helmet. 'Your face is filthy.'

'I'll wash it when I get to my first patient,' she said dismissively, and he shook his head.

'No you won't,' he said. 'You are not riding around the country looking as though you've been in a fire. I have a handkerchief, and some water in my car. I'll clean you up.'

'But—'

'Dr Lorimer, you are going to let me clean you up,' he declared, 'or you're heading straight back to the surgery.'

She stuck out her tongue at him. 'You're a bully, you know that, don't you?'

'Alex.'

'OK—OK,' she said, resignation plain on her face, 'but can you make it fast or your patients will be starting to organise a search party for me.'

He tried to make it fast but he would have been a lot quicker if she hadn't kept twisting her mouth around.

'Will you keep still?' he exclaimed as she jerked her chin out of his hand once again.

'Hugh, this is my face, not a brick,' she protested. 'You're scrubbing too hard.'

'Wimp,' he said.

'Am not,' she retorted mulishly.

She wasn't, he thought as he clasped her chin again, and began to rub more gently, but she definitely needed a minder. Somebody to watch out for her, someone who would make sure she didn't do anything dumb, and it looked like it was going to have to be him. Malcolm was too busy, and her boyfriend was God knows where, so it would have to be him or heaven knows what mess she would get herself into. OK, so she would undoubtedly chop him off at the knees if she knew what he was thinking, but she was his locum, his responsibility.

'Aren't you finished yet?' she said, and he shook his head at her.

'You've no patience, have you?'

'Yeah, right, and like you have?' she replied, and he chuckled.

She had such fine features, he thought, as he rubbed at a particularly stubborn patch of oil on her cheek, such very delicate bones. Jenny hadn't been fine-boned. She'd been a woman, with a woman's curves, but Alex…

She was definitely a water sprite. A water sprite with such very pale skin. A water sprite with enormous green eyes, and, as Hugh stared down at her, he forgot the handkerchief he was holding. Forgot everything as all sound faded, and the world seemed to slip away, leaving just the two of them, until he saw her eyes change from impatience, to confusion, and then— just for a second—to something that caused his heart to in- explicably tighten in his chest before she quickly stepped back from him.

'I…I have to go, Hugh,' she mumbled. 'The patients… My home visits…'

'Right.' He nodded. 'Your face… I didn't mean it to take so long. I just….'

Just what? he wondered. One minute he'd been trying to get the oil off her skin, thinking she needed a minder, and the next…

'It was my fault,' she muttered. 'I wouldn't stand still. I…' She backed up another step. 'I really do have to go.'

'Me, too,' he said, not moving at all, but when she pulled on her helmet he couldn't help but add, 'Alex, all these locum posts you take… Why don't you accept one of the partner- ships you've been offered?'

She shrugged. 'Itchy feet, I guess.'

'Yes, but…'

He couldn't have said any more if he'd wanted to. She had already closed her visor, effectively shutting him out, and when she hit her ignition the roar of her bike prevented any further conversation.

'Drive carefully,' he shouted, but she didn't even nod.

She just rode off, leaving him staring after her.

There was more to it than itchy feet, he thought as he walked slowly back to his car. In fact, he suspected there was a whole lot more to Alex Lorimer than she ever let the world see. She was a puzzle, and no mistake. Just as that very odd feeling he'd experienced when he'd been cleaning her face had been a puzzle.

Post-traumatic stress, he told himself dismissively. When people were put into dangerous situations, the relief of surviving them often made them feel strange, not quite themselves. It was easily explained, easily accounted for, but Alex Lorimer… She really *was* a puzzle.

CHAPTER THREE

ALEX frowned as she gently examined Jamie Allen's elbow. She could see a very definite swelling, with quite a bit of discolouration. The six-year-old hadn't been able to bend his elbow, and when she'd tried to do it for him he'd let out a yelp of pain.

'He could simply have badly jarred it,' Alex said, sitting back on her heels, and staring up at the boy's mother, 'but I have to say I think it's more likely he's got a supracondylar humerus fracture—a fractured elbow. He fell out of a tree, you said?'

Grace Allen nodded.

'He was pretending to be a Power Ranger,' she replied. 'In the spring he broke his ankle when he fell off the garden shed pretending to be a spy. I tell you, Doctor, he's only six, but he's broken more bones since he was born than his seven brothers put together.'

'You like climbing, Jamie?' Alex said, shifting her attention back to the little boy, and he grinned back at her with the kind of impish wide-eyed expression that Alex knew from experience generally spelt trouble.

'I want to be an astronaut when I grow up,' he replied, 'or a tightrope walker.'

'Always supposing he lives that long,' his mother said ruefully. 'So it's off to the hospital for an X-ray, is it, Doctor?'

Alex nodded. 'They'll probably X-ray both of Jamie's elbows because it can be quite hard sometimes to tell whether someone so young has sustained a fracture. If there's what we call a "fat-pad" visible on the X-ray, then it's definitely a fracture. If there isn't—'

'It'll be a fracture,' Grace Allen interrupted with resignation. 'It always is with Jamie. At least he's so accustomed now to plaster casts that he just takes them in his stride. When he had pneumonia last year, we had the devil's own job trying to get him to take the medication.'

'You don't like taking pills, Jamie?' Alex said, smiling at the little boy, and he shook his head vigorously.

'They always taste like sheep droppings.'

'*Jamie.*'

'It's all right, Mrs Allen.' Alex laughed, seeing the mortification on the woman's face. 'Shall I tell you something, Jamie?' she said, leaning towards him conspiratorially. 'I don't like taking pills either. I needed to take quite a few some years back and I thought they tasted like sheep droppings, too.'

'Do you still have to take them?' Jamie asked, and Alex nodded.

'Not the sheep droppings ones, thankfully, but I do need to take some.' *Too much information, Alex,* she thought, suddenly realising that Mrs Allen was staring at her curiously. *You're giving away far too much information.* 'How's Ewan doing?' she said, quickly changing the subject, and Mrs Allen smiled.

'They moved him out of Intensive Care yesterday. He'll be in the hospital for at least another five weeks, but the consultant says he should make a full recovery in time. I still can't thank you enough for what you did, Doctor,' Mrs Allen continued. 'Dr Hugh told me if it wasn't for you, Ewan wouldn't have survived the crash.'

'Dr Hugh exaggerated,' Alex said firmly. 'It was a team effort.'

'I know what I know,' the woman said. 'Did Neil bring in the box of groceries for you?'

'He did, but there was no need for you to give me a present, Mrs Allen,' Alex replied. *And especially not the live chicken.* 'I did no more than my job.'

'Which doesn't mean I can't show my appreciation,' Mrs Allen said, getting heavily to her feet, then glancing down at her son. 'Come on, you wee rapscallion. We're off to the hospital again, but I'll see you next week, Doctor. I'm coming to your slimming classes,' she continued as Alex stared at her in surprise. 'It's about time I lost some weight, and your classes sound fun.'

Alex hoped they would be as she walked Mrs Allen through to the waiting room, then waved goodbye. She'd thought long and hard about how she could kick-start the classes back into life, and making them fun seemed the best way.

'What's young Jamie broken now?'

Alex turned to see Hugh standing behind her, and smiled.

'His elbow,' she said, 'but I gather from Mrs Allen that he's quite accident prone.'

'And how. He's broken a leg, a collarbone, an ankle, an arm and a wrist up to now.'

Alex frowned slightly. 'You don't think he could possibly have—'

'Osteogenesis imperfecta?' Hugh shook his head. 'After his second fracture I had him tested for brittle bone disease, but his scans were clear. He's just never happier than when he's climbing, and I'm afraid his enthusiasm is better than his balance and he keeps falling.'

'I don't know how Mrs Allen is still sane after having brought up eight sons,' Alex declared. 'Are all of them blond like Ewan, Jamie and Neil?'

'Every single one of them.' Hugh shot her a speculative glance. 'I hear Neil was back in again yesterday. I've seen him just once in the past ten years, and now he appears to virtually haunt the place.'

'Thank goodness he doesn't bring a live chicken with him every time he comes,' Alex said with feeling. 'Did you manage to find a good home for it?'

'The very best,' Hugh replied. 'It's in the butcher's freezer ready for you to collect whenever you want.'

'It's in…?' She stared at him, open-mouthed for a second, then a bubble of horrified laughter sprang from her. 'Hugh, that is *gross*.'

'It's practical,' he protested. 'Of course, if you would rather have kept it, bought it a lead, called it Rupert…?'

'You know perfectly well that I wouldn't,' she exclaimed. 'But when I asked you to find it a good home I was thinking of a farm, or a croft.'

'It would have ended up in a pot eventually,' he said, 'so it might as well be yours.'

'I guess so.'

He shot her another glance. 'Just as I'm sure you also know why Neil has suddenly become a regular feature at our surgery over the past fortnight.'

'He can save his journeys as far as I'm concerned,' she said firmly. 'I'm not interested.'

'Even though he's blond, blue-eyed, personable, and owns his own garage?'

'Neil Allen could own the whole of the north of Scotland and I still wouldn't be interested.'

'Then what about Rory Murray?' Hugh observed, his grey eyes gleaming. 'You wouldn't believe the number of times he's turned up to have his hip checked, and he's always extremely disappointed when Chrissie sends him through to me. OK, so he's ten years older than Neil, and doesn't have blond hair, but he's a plumber, and plumbers earn more than doctors do nowadays.'

Alex fixed him with a beady glare. 'You know, you're asking for a slap.'

'You'd give me one, too, wouldn't you?' Hugh laughed. 'Just three referral letters to type this afternoon, Chrissie,' he added as the receptionist joined them. 'One for orthopaedics, one for dermatology—and, yes, I do know I'll probably be receiving my pension by the time we get an appointment for that department,' he continued as Chrissie groaned, 'and one appointment for ENT.'

'What is it with dermatology departments?' Alex asked. 'No matter what part of the country I've worked in, I can guarantee it will take for ever to get a patient an appointment with them.'

'They say there aren't enough of them,' Hugh replied. 'We say they should pull their collective fingers out.'

'Talking of collective fingers,' Chrissie declared, 'Malcolm phoned to say don't wait for him but to just go ahead with the post-surgery debriefing. He doesn't know when he'll be back from his home visits. He has an extra call to make. To Lady Soutar.'

It was Hugh's turn to groan.

'I take it Lady Soutar is bad news?' Alex observed, glancing from Hugh to Chrissie. 'I've not met her yet—'

'You will,' Hugh interrupted. 'She owns Glen Dhu lodge, plus 40,000 acres of deer, salmon and trout, and she's…difficult.'

'You mean I'll probably need therapy after I've visited her,' Alex said, and Hugh grinned.

'I'd bet money on it.' He glanced down at his watch. 'Debriefing in my room in ten minutes if that's OK with you?'

She nodded, and as Hugh strode away Alex became aware

that Chrissie was observing her with a singularly smug expression.

'Told you he was a good man, didn't I?' the reception-ist declared.

'OK—all right—I was wrong, and I admit it,' Alex replied. 'He's a nice man when you get to know him.'

'And you've got him laughing,' Chrissie continued. 'Malcolm was just saying the other morning that he hasn't seen Hugh laugh so much in years.'

'Yup, regular circus clown act, that's me,' Alex said lightly, and Chrissie shook her head at her.

'I mean it, Alex, you're good for him—'

'Hey, hold on there a minute,' Alex interrupted. 'If you're thinking what I think you're thinking...'

'I meant the practice,' Chrissie said hurriedly, her cheeks darkening. 'You're good for the practice.'

'It's already a good practice,' Alex said. 'All it needs is another doctor. You can't run it with just two—your patients are too scattered.'

Chrissie nodded, then cleared her throat.

'I don't suppose you'd consider staying on here when your contract's up? It's a really nice place to live,' the receptionist continued quickly as Alex began to shake her head. 'You can leave your front door open, your car keys in the ignition, and if you've got kids they can roam about in perfect safety.'

'Number one, Hugh is going to want somebody a whole lot more experienced than me for a full-time post,' Alex re-plied. 'Number two, I have plans and staying on here isn't one of them, and number three, a place like this is really only great if you're married with kids.'

'And you don't plan to do either?'

'Nope.'

And she didn't, Alex thought as she went back into her consulting room to collect her notebook. She would never marry, and as for children…

Her heart twisted slightly and unconsciously she put her fingers to her cheek. How long had it been since she'd been touched by a man? Jonathan had walked away almost four years ago. But it wasn't Jonathan's touch that she couldn't forget.

It was Hugh Scott, scrubbing away at her face for all he was worth, clearly thinking she was a lunatic, until he'd suddenly stopped. He'd just stood there, cupping her chin in his hand, and she'd been about to make a joke, to say, *Come on, dozy daydream,* when his quicksilver eyes had caught hers, and, without warning, her heart had suddenly filled with such longing, with such an inexplicable yearning, that she'd wanted to walk straight into his arms, and stay there.

Which was crazy. OK, so she liked him—more than liked him if she was honest with herself-but she was just passing through.

Hugh Scott doesn't even realise you're a woman, her mind pointed out, and she let out a shuddering sigh. To him, she was simply a colleague, someone who made him laugh, and it was better that way. It really was, because she couldn't stay here. Her life, her decision, and yet…

'Alex, Hugh says are you coming to the post-surgery debriefing any time soon?' Chrissie declared as she stuck her head round her consulting-room door, and Alex smiled ruefully.

'Tell him I'm on my way,' she said, lifting her notebook. 'And tell him I'm sorry.'

She was, too, she realised as the receptionist disappeared. Sorry for a lot of things, but regrets never got anyone anywhere, and with an effort she pasted her everything's-wonderful-in-my-world expression onto her face, and headed for Hugh's consulting room.

* * *

'So, any worries or concerns about any of the patients you saw this afternoon?' Hugh declared, leaning back in his seat, cradling his coffee in his hands.

'One concern, one worry,' Alex replied. 'I had a biker in who's camping with friends out by Inverannan. He'd forgotten to bring his tranquillisers on holiday with him, and he wasn't very happy when I said I would have to contact his GP before I could give him a prescription, so I was wondering if I was a bit overcautious?'

'Not at all. Visitors—holidaymakers—often turn up at the surgery having forgotten to pack their medication, and if it's something run-of-the-mill I generally make out a prescription for them, but if it's for narcotics or tranquillisers I always contact their GP. Was that the concern or the worry?'

'The concern,' Alex said. 'Ellie Dickson's my worry. She came in to have her BP checked, and I noticed on her file that she developed pre-eclampsia when she was expecting her first baby. She's now almost six and a half months pregnant with her second child, but it's two months since her last check-up, and when I mentioned it to her she simply said she'd been busy.'

'Ellie would say that,' Hugh said grimly. 'How was her BP?'

'Perfect,' Alex replied. 'I just don't like the idea of her not coming back for another couple of months.'

'Neither do I,' Hugh said. 'I'll have a word with her husband, Geordie, on the quiet, see if he can make her see sense.'

'I saw Donna Ferguson going into your consulting room,' Alex declared, and Hugh's expression grew even grimmer.

'She's feeling constantly tired all the time now, Alex. The lab tests revealed that she has slightly higher than normal blood sugar levels which would suggest Type II diabetes, but her symptoms…' He shook his head. 'There's something else. I know it, feel it.'

'If she does have late onset diabetes, it's certainly easy to treat,' Alex said encouragingly. 'She would simply need to adjust her diet, making sure she eats regularly, and watches her carbohydrate intake.'

'*If* she has Type II diabetes.'

She nodded. 'If.'

He looked worried and depressed. She supposed it was inevitable he should become personally involved with patients as he'd been in the area for so long, but she didn't like to see him looking down, and he suddenly looked very down.

'What can you tell me about Frank and Irene Nolan?' she said, deliberately changing the subject.

He frowned, clearly trying to place the names.

'Married couple in their mid-forties, bought Heatherlea croft four months ago,' he murmured. 'I've seen him out and about occasionally, but not her. They haven't signed on with the practice yet, so I haven't met either of them professionally.'

'That's a bit odd, don't you think?' Alex said. 'Not having signed on with a doctor when they've been here for four months?'

'A lot of people like to get settled in first,' Hugh replied, 'and if both of the Nolans are in good health, signing on with a doctor probably doesn't seem a top priority.' A frown appeared on Alex's forehead, and he gazed at her quizzically. 'You think there's a problem?'

'I don't know,' Alex admitted. 'I met them yesterday when I was on my way back from my home visits. I'd stopped on the road to take a breather, and they were out walking. I said hello, and then I noticed Mrs Nolan had a bad cut on her forehead so I told her she should come down to the surgery to have it dressed.'

'And?'

Alex smiled ruefully. 'She told me to mind my own business.'

Hugh sat back in his seat. 'Country people can be difficult, Alex. Sometimes you have to bully them into getting medical treatment, sometimes you have to coax them. How bad was her cut?'

'It'll heal up OK, if she doesn't get dirt in it, but she had some bruises on her face as well as the cut,' Alex continued. 'Older bruises, as though she either falls a lot or...'

'You're thinking her husband hits her?' Hugh asked, and Alex bit her lip.

'She didn't seem cowed, and he was actually incredibly solicitous towards her, but you know how in the country people will normally talk you to death until they find out everything they can about you? I got the distinct impression the Nolans wanted rid of me.'

'Alex, we can't force people to come in for treatment,' Hugh observed, 'particularly if they're not a patient. I can certainly drop in on them when I'm next in the area, introduce myself, check out the situation, but if Irene Nolan doesn't want to come and see us—'

'Who doesn't want to come and see us?' Malcolm interrupted, looking tired and grumpy as he walked into Hugh's consulting room.

'Irene Nolan,' Hugh replied, and Malcolm shook his head.

'Never heard of her,' he said.

'Probably because we haven't seen her in a professional capacity,' Hugh said. 'She and her husband bought Heatherlea farm about four months ago. Alex thinks there's something odd about them.'

'And Hugh thinks I'm overreacting,' Alex declared, getting to her feet. 'And on that note I'm going back to my room to finish writing up my notes and then I'm going home for dinner.'

Malcolm waited until the door had safely closed behind Alex, then he turned suspiciously to Hugh.

'Have you two had a row?'

'Of course we haven't,' Hugh exclaimed. 'Alex thinks the Nolans are strange, and I suspect they simply don't welcome strangers. How was Lady Soutar?'

Malcolm rolled his eyes. 'Lady Soutar was…Lady Soutar.'

Hugh grinned. 'Maybe we should send Alex out to see her next time. That would be an interesting consultation.'

'It would certainly be explosive.' Malcolm bounced for a second on the balls of his feet. 'Have you seen the poster re-advertising the slimming and exercise club?'

'Alex told me she was restarting the classes next week,' Hugh replied. 'I hope some women turn up for it—and I mean that. I remember the problems Jenny had at the beginning—'

'I don't think Alex is going to have difficulty getting women to turn up,' Malcolm broke in. 'In fact, I think it's going to be more a case of how she is going to fit everybody in. Chrissie's going, so is Mrs Allen, Peggie Fraser, Ellie Dickson, Sybil Gordon—'

'Oh, God, has she resurfaced?' Hugh groaned. 'What's the betting her next ailment is repetitive strain syndrome from all the bending and stretching?'

Malcolm cleared his throat. 'I take it you haven't seen the poster in the waiting room?'

'Malcolm, I don't have time to stare at posters in the waiting room,' Hugh said irritably. 'Is there a problem with Alex's class?'

Malcolm opened his mouth, then closed it again.

'I think maybe you should take a look at the poster.'

Hugh stared at the poster on the waiting room wall for a long moment, then turned to Malcolm.

'She's got to be kidding.'

'I suppose it *is* exercising…'

'But *belly dancing*?' Hugh exclaimed. 'Malcolm, this is

Kilbreckan, not Cairo. The women in the area are crofter and fishermen's wives, and the thought of them belly dancing... The mind boggles.'

'Mine certainly does when I picture Sybil Gordon doing it.'

'Oh, Jeez, yes,' Hugh gasped, then started to laugh. 'She's insane—absolutely insane.'

'Who is?'

Malcolm and Hugh turned to see Alex standing behind them, and Malcolm crimsoned.

'Nobody you know. Hugh and I— We were— I mean—'

'We were talking about you, Alex,' Hugh said, coming to his partner's rescue. 'These classes you're starting next week. I'm not saying they're a bad idea,' he continued hurriedly, seeing Alex's eyes narrow. 'Any kind of exercise is bound to be good—but belly dancing... For a start, Sybil Gordon is fifty-eight and very overweight.'

'Belly dancing is for all ages, shapes and fitness levels,' Alex replied firmly. 'It doesn't put any more stress on your body than a brisk walk, so if Sybil Gordon is fit enough to walk, and to wiggle her bottom in front of her bathroom mirror, she's fit enough to take a class.'

'OK, but won't the women who come to the class need to buy...' Hugh desperately tried to blot out a mental image of Sybil Gordon wearing a glittery bra and harem pants, and wiggling her bottom anywhere. 'Particular clothes. There's not a lot of money in the area.'

'Nobody has to buy anything special—I've emphasised that on the poster,' she exclaimed. 'The women who turn up only need to bring a scarf they can tie round their hips so they can see their own hip movements.'

'But what about Ellie Dickson?' Hugh said, all too aware that he was losing this argument, but determined to make a stand nevertheless. 'Should she be doing any sort of dancing at her stage in pregnancy?'

'Pregnancy isn't a disease,' Alex protested, 'and belly dancing was actually used as prenatal conditioning for women in ancient times because it helped strengthen the pelvic muscles.'

'Yes, but—'

'Hugh, I've been taking belly dancing classes for almost four years,' Alex insisted, 'and I know there are some movements that should be avoided if you're pregnant. No way will I let Ellie attempt the belly ripple, the pelvic tilt or any shimmies, but she'll be perfectly safe with the lulling, calming movements and, in fact, they could actually give her an easier birth when her time comes.'

'I'm sorry, but you lost me after the words "belly ripple",' he said, and Alex thrust the folders she was carrying into Malcolm's arms.

'This is a belly ripple,' she said. 'Keeping your back almost straight, you make a "wave" backward and forward with your pelvis like this so you get an undulating, rippling effect. Obviously you'd see the effect better if I was in costume,' she added, taking her folders back from Malcolm who was gazing at her with a slightly bemused expression, 'but you get the general picture.'

Hugh didn't. Maybe the movement had lost some of its impact because Alex was wearing her customary baggy sweatshirt and jeans, but he'd always thought belly dancing was supposed to be sexy, but either he was dead from the neck down, or it was vastly overrated, because, to him, what Alex had done simply looked weird.

'Alex—'

'Look, if you're worried about the safety aspect,' she interrupted, 'why don't you drop in on the first class, check it out for yourself?'

Wild horses wouldn't have dragged Hugh in to watch Sybil Gordon attempting to perform a belly ripple, or circle, or whatever it was that Alex had called it, but he had no intention of saying so.

'It depends on how busy I am,' he said vaguely, and before Alex could pin him down to a definite yes, he added, 'And now I'm off home. I'm on call tonight, and I'd like to get something to eat before the phone starts ringing.'

Belly dancing, Hugh thought ruefully as he poured himself a whisky, then walked over to his sofa, slipping off his jacket as he went. How in the world had Alex ever come up with that idea? Jenny would never have suggested it in a million years, but then Jenny had always been such a calm, practical person, whereas Alex...He chuckled as he sipped his drink. He never knew what she was going to do next. It was like standing next to a firecracker, wondering which direction it was going to go off, but Jenny would have liked her.

He did, too. He liked her ready wit, her can-do attitude. He was even getting used to her hair, though he still thought it would have looked nicer if it hadn't been quite so short.

She has beautiful eyes, his mind whispered as he finished his drink, and she did. They were so very green, like sparkling emeralds, but he'd also occasionally seen dark shadows lurking in them. Shadows he recognised because they'd been in his own eyes after Jenny died. Something, or someone, had hurt Alex badly in the past, and he didn't like to think of her being hurt, or being in trouble, he thought as he heard a tentative knock on his sitting-room door and knew it could only be one person.

'I'm really sorry to bother you,' Alex said, looking awkward and uncomfortable when he opened the door. 'I know it's an imposition—you don't like being disturbed—and I wouldn't have come, except—'

'It's OK—really—you didn't disturb me,' he insisted, remembering all too forcefully what he'd said to her on her first night in Kilbreckan. 'What's wrong?'

'I've no water.'

'Water?' he repeated blankly and she nodded.

'Liquid stuff, H_2O, normally comes out of taps, or in my case it doesn't—isn't—or at least not out of the hot-water tap.'

'Sounds like you could have an air lock,' he said, going to the cupboard in his hall and pulling out a box of tools.

'And you know how to fix it?' she said with clear surprise.

'If you've lived in the country as long as I have,' he declared as he began to climb the stairs, 'you very quickly learn—if you want to survive—how to become proficient in minor household tasks.'

'This should be interesting,' she said as she followed him into her flat, and he shook his head at her over his shoulder.

'Oh, ye of little faith. Look, if this doesn't work,' he continued, pulling a small length of hose out of his box, and sliding one end over each tap, then securing them with metal clips, 'I promise I'll get Rory Murray round here with bribery if necessary, although he's so smitten with you I doubt he'd need bribing.'

Quickly he turned on the cold water, there was a whooshing, gurgling noise, then he turned off the cold water, removed the hose from the taps, and, when he turned both taps on again, water flowed out of both.

'I'm impressed,' Alex said. 'No, seriously, I am,' she continued as his left eyebrow rose, 'and best of all you saved me from Rory Murray.'

'You need saving from Rory Murray?' he said, and she gave him a hard stare.

'What do you think?' she said, and Hugh laughed.

'I think if Rory tried anything on, you'd wrap a piece of hosepipe round his neck, and stuff washers up his nose.'

'Too darn right,' she said with a gurgle of laughter. 'Look, I was just about to eat when I discovered I had no hot water. Do you want to join me, by way of a thank you? It's nothing fancy, just some salad and cold chicken.'

'It's not Rupert, is it?' he said, his grey eyes dancing.

'No, it's not Rupert,' she said reprovingly. 'Please stay. There's more than enough for two.'

'I'd like that,' he said, and she smiled.

'It will be ready in about five minutes, so why don't you make yourself at home in the sitting room?'

He would, he thought, if the sitting room hadn't been quite so depressing. Funny how he'd never noticed that before when the other locums had been staying here, but he noticed it now.

The only sign that this was a home was the framed photograph on the mantelpiece and curiously he picked it up, then his lips curved. He would have recognised the girl in the picture anywhere. She was younger—maybe about twenty-four or twenty-five—and her red hair was long—right past her shoulders—but it was indisputably Alex, flanked by a woman with short red hair and a man with grey hair.

'Is this your mum and dad?' he said when Alex came back into the sitting room carrying two heavily laden plates, and she nodded.

'It was taken five years ago, and it's my favourite picture of them. My dad… He had a stroke and died a month after the photo was taken.'

'I'm sorry.'

'It was rough at the time,' she said, setting down the plates and some cutlery on the small dining table. 'He was a great dad, and I loved him very much.'

'You had your hair long then,' he said.

She took the photograph from him, and put it back on the mantelpiece.

'It became a nuisance,' she said abruptly, 'so I had it cut short about four years ago.'

He wished she hadn't, but it hardly seemed polite to say so.

'Do you have any brothers or sisters?' he said instead, and she shook her head.

'I'm an only child. In fact, my mother had all but given up hope of ever becoming pregnant when I came along.'

'So she spoilt you rotten,' he observed.

She tilted her head quizzically. 'I don't know. Do you reckon she did?'

He didn't think she was spoilt. A bit headstrong, perhaps, a little stubborn, but he didn't think she was spoilt.

'Your silence is pretty telling,' she pointed out and his lips quirked.

'Well, if the cap fits…'

'I think we should eat,' she said, and he grinned.

'This looks good,' he said as he sat down at the dining table.

'It's easy, and I'm very much a fan of easy when it comes to cooking.'

'But not when it comes to slimming classes,' he observed, lifting his knife and fork. 'What in the world made you decide that belly dancing was what Kilbreckan needed?'

'Dieting and exercising are boring, Hugh,' she exclaimed. 'So I thought how can I make this fun, and belly dancing seemed to fit the bill.'

'Malcolm says the interest has been phenomenal,' he observed, 'but I can't understand why you ever learned. You don't need to lose weight. In fact, I'd say you could do with putting some weight on.'

Quite a bit of weight on, he thought, as she reached for a piece of bread, and he saw how very thin her wrists were.

'Belly dancing was one of my challenges,' she replied.

'Your challenges?' he repeated, and she smiled.

'You know how people make New Year resolutions?' she said. 'Well, about four years ago I started making New Year challenges, and each New Year I decide what I want to learn, or to do, and one year it was belly dancing.'

'I suppose it could have been worse,' he said as he forked some chicken into his mouth. 'You could have suggested all the overweight women in Kilbreckan take up skydiving.'

'It's certainly good exercise.'

He blinked. 'You've been skydiving?'

'And white water rafting, and hang-gliding.'

'And the reason would be?' he demanded, and it was her turn to blink.

'The reason for what?'

'Taking up sports that no sane person would ever even contemplate. They're all dangerous, Alex.'

In fact, the thought of her doing any of those things was enough to make his blood run cold, but Alex clearly didn't agree with him. In fact, she looked irritated.

'Crossing the road is dangerous,' she exclaimed, pointing her fork at him. 'Actually—statistically—crossing the road is a lot more dangerous.'

'Yes, but—'

'I just want to live life to the full, Hugh, to not miss out on any opportunities, to see everything there is to see. We only come this way once, remember?'

'Agreed,' he argued back, 'which is why most normal people want to go to Venice to stand in St Mark's Square, or to the US to ride through the Grand Canyon or to climb the

Statue of Liberty. They don't want to throw themselves out of planes, or fling themselves down rapids.'

'I don't fling, or throw, myself out of anything,' she protested. 'I always make sure I follow all the safety procedures. I think it's great you're content with where you are, what you do, but for me…There's a whole world of opportunities out there, and I want to try as many of them as I can.'

'Which is why you take all these locum jobs,' he said with dawning comprehension. 'So you can save some money, then head off again to complete one of your challenges.'

'Exactly,' she said. 'Maybe one day—when I've seen everything, done everything I want to do—I might stop moving around, but…' She shrugged. 'Who knows?'

'And what does your boyfriend think about all the things you get up to?' he asked before he could stop himself, only to add hurriedly, 'Sorry, that was a very personal question. Forget I asked.'

'It's OK,' she said, her eyes not meeting his. 'I don't have a boyfriend. I was engaged once, but…'

'It didn't work out?'

Tell him, a small voice insisted in Alex's head. *He'll understand, and when you leave in a couple of months he'll see it's nothing personal, that it's just the way things are, so tell him.*

'Alex?'

He was waiting for her to reply, his grey eyes fixed on her, and she took a deep breath.

'Jonathan and I met at a party when I was at med school. He was—still is for all I know—a stockbroker, and I fell for him pretty hard. We got engaged, and then…' *Say it, Alex, say it*. 'I found out…I found out…'

'He wasn't the man you wanted to spend the rest of your life with?' Hugh finished for her gently, and to her surprise, he put down his knife and fork, and reached for her hand.

'You'll find the right man one day, Alex. Jonathan was an idiot to let you go, but you'll find the right man, and live happily ever after and have lots of beautiful babies.'

You don't know how wrong you are, she thought, feeling her heart squeeze tight inside her, and she wanted to tell him why he was wrong but his hand felt so good holding hers, and if she told him he would hold on to it out of pity, and she didn't want that.

'I…I guess so,' she managed. 'Can I ask you a personal question?'

'It depends on what it is.' His expression was suddenly wary.

'How did you meet Jenny?'

For a second she didn't think he was going to answer, then he smiled.

'I was at a GP conference five years ago and during the interval this really boring guy collared me, and I was desperately trying to think of some excuse to get away from him, and suddenly she was there.'

'She was pretty?' Alex said wistfully, seeing his face soften as he spoke.

'She was beautiful. She said, "I'm terribly sorry, but you're needed urgently Dr Scott." She'd read my name tag, you see,' he continued, his eyes dark with the memory, 'and when she'd got me away she laughed and said, "I thought you needed rescuing."'

'And that was it,' Alex said. 'You fell for her, hook, line and sinker.'

'Totally.' He nodded. 'We got married six weeks later, and though we only had three years together before…before she was killed, we shared so much. Not just the love we felt for each other, but we had the same taste in books, and in music, and she…she was a friend. I know that sounds stupid—'

'No, it doesn't,' she said, her throat constricted.

'But now she's gone and…' He let go of her hand, his face unbearably bleak and desolate. 'I'm nothing without her. I just get through the days as best I can, trying not to think, not to remember. She was so special, Alex, and everything I'm not. Kind, and patient, and gentle.'

'You can be kind, too,' she pointed out, her heart aching for him, wishing he hadn't let go of her hand so she could hold his, could comfort him in some way. 'OK, so you're not the most patient man in the world but I've never seen you brusque with a patient.'

'I was before you joined us,' he said ruefully. 'Malcolm threatened to relegate me to the paperwork if I didn't keep a lid on my temper.'

'You were probably just tired,' she insisted. 'There's too much work here for two doctors, you need another partner.'

'I know, but…Malcolm keeps telling me to move on, that I should let go, but… All my life I've been on the outside looking in, Alex. Maybe it's because my parents moved around a lot when I was a kid. Maybe it's because I was an only child like you and never learned how to connect with people.' He shrugged awkwardly. 'I don't know, but when I met Jenny…'

'When you met Jenny?' she prompted, and his mouth twisted.

'She brought me in from the cold, made me feel for the first time like I belonged. With her I wasn't on the outside any more, with her I felt whole and complete, and when she died…' He took a shuddering breath. 'Everything that meant anything to me died, too.'

'You'll find someone else, Hugh,' Alex said through a throat so tight it hurt. 'There's someone out there for you who can heal your heart, I know there is.'

'No, there isn't,' he said sadly, 'because, you see, I'm a for-ever man. I loved Jenny so much—I always will, so, you see…'

She did see, she thought, as she saw the heartbreak in his

face, just as she also realised that for the first time in her life she was actually envious of a dead woman.

What must it feel like to be loved so utterly and completely? She'd thought Jonathan had loved her but he had never once looked at her the way Hugh was looking now as he remembered his dead wife. Never once made it so clear that she was his whole heart, and soul, and she had to swallow hard to ease the hard lump that had formed in her throat.

'Hugh—'

'I'm sorry,' he said with a shaky laugh. 'Unburdening myself like this…I shouldn't have—I don't know why I did.'

'I think—perhaps—you needed to talk to someone,' she said softly. 'That maybe it was long overdue.'

'Maybe.' He shifted awkwardly in his seat. 'So, who do you confide in, tell your troubles to?'

She couldn't tell him now. She couldn't ever tell him. He'd been through so much, was still hurting so much, and to land all her problems on him when she was just passing through… It wouldn't be fair, and it wouldn't be right.

'Don't have any troubles,' she said lightly. 'Don't need to confide in anybody.'

He didn't believe her, and she knew he didn't, and so she talked about their patients, told him that the biker who had wanted a prescription for tranquillisers had given her a bogus telephone number for his GP, and was relieved when his cellphone rang and he had to go.

But, after he'd gone, she walked over to the mantelpiece and picked up the photograph. None of them had known what the future would bring when that picture was taken. None of them could possibly have guessed that their whole lives would soon be torn apart. Life was so fragile. It could trickle through your fingers like grains of sand, and there would be no happyever-after for her despite what Hugh had said.

There couldn't even be a happy-just-for-the-moment time with Hugh, she thought, her lips twisting into a sad parody of a smile as she put the photograph back down. I'm a forever man, he'd said, and he was, so she'd get through the next few weeks as best she could, then leave and concentrate on her next goal because in her goals was certainty. The only certainty she would ever have.

CHAPTER FOUR

'I'M SORRY, Dr Hugh, so sorry!' Donna Ferguson exclaimed as he pressed a handkerchief into her hand, and she used it to wipe the tears from her eyes. 'Breaking down like this—embarrassing you—'

'You are not embarrassing me,' Hugh interrupted firmly. 'You're feeling wretched and miserable, and if I was in your situation I'd be howling my eyes out, too.'

Donna let out a hiccuping laugh. 'I doubt that, but... What's *wrong* with me, Doctor? I know I've only been on the diet you gave me for a week, but I feel like I've got even less energy now than I had before, and look at my fingers. They're like big, fat sausages, and I've started getting awful cramps in my stomach now, too.'

Hugh kept his sympathetic expression in place, but he groaned inwardly. The minute Donna Ferguson walked into his consulting room he'd known she was getting worse rather than better on the diet he'd prescribed, and though a change of diet often took a little while to take effect she should have felt some improvement.

'Have you noticed your skin becoming drier than normal, Donna?' he asked.

She shook her head.

'Are you putting on weight, perhaps noticing your hair is getting thinner?'

'I weigh just the same as I always do, and my hair doesn't feel any different.' Donna looked alarmed. 'What are you thinking, Doctor?'

'I'm wondering whether you might perhaps have an underactive thyroid,' he said. 'The thyroid is a gland in your neck that helps regulate your energy levels. Some of your symptoms…' *unfortunately not all of them* '…could suggest your thyroid isn't working properly.'

'Then you don't think I have the Type II diabetes you suspected last week, Doctor?'

Hugh sighed.

'To be honest, Donna, I don't know what's wrong with you so I'd like to take some more blood and urine samples.'

Donna Ferguson didn't look happy, and Hugh didn't blame her. He wouldn't have been happy either if the person he'd been expecting to give him a diagnosis seemed incapable of coming up with one. The trouble was Donna's symptoms could fit any number of conditions, and all he could do was systematically work through them. A situation that was as disheartening for Donna as it was frustrating for him.

'Anybody else in the waiting room, Chrissie?' he asked after Donna had left and he'd deposited her samples in the receptionist's out-tray.

'Not a soul,' she replied, then tilted her head sympathetically. 'Rough morning?'

'You could say that. Is Malcolm still here?'

Chrissie's cheeks dimpled. 'He headed off very reluctantly about half an hour ago, muttering the whole way.'

'It's only fair he goes to the in-service seminar at the hospital,' Hugh protested. 'I had to endure it last time.'

'I know, but he was still unhappy,' Chrissie replied. 'He

wanted to be here for the first of Alex's slimming and exercise classes this evening. Are you coming to it?'

'Depends on how far I get with the paperwork,' Hugh said vaguely.

And if I can manage to slip away without Alex dragging me in to experience the joys of Sybil Gordon attempting to belly dance, he added mentally.

Except he wasn't one hundred per cent certain that Alex *would* drag him in. All week she'd seemed...

Not quite herself were the only words he could come up with, and even they weren't accurate. She was hitting the ground running with her patients as she always did, and contributing to the post-surgery meetings as usual, but he'd thought her laughter had sounded slightly strained this week, almost forced, and there'd been times when he'd caught a wistful, almost sad look on her face. A look that had instantly disappeared the minute she'd sensed his gaze on her.

'Is Alex ready for the post-surgery debriefing?' he said and Chrissie shook her head.

'She's still with her last patient. It's Neil Allen, and he seems to have hurt his foot quite badly judging from the way he was limping.'

The garage owner was also making rather a large meal out of it, Hugh thought irritably, as the young man came out of Alex's consulting room, and he saw the way he was leaning heavily on her, and his arm was round her shoulders.

'Hugh, can you reinforce what I've just been saying to Neil?' Alex said the minute she saw him. 'He stepped on a rusty nail in his garage, but not only did he not come to see us about it, he also hasn't been keeping his tetanus shots up to date, so he now has a pretty severe infection.'

'I see,' Hugh declared.

So, too, did Neil, he thought with satisfaction, because

under his steady gaze the garage owner's smile had disappeared and he'd removed his arm from Alex's shoulders.

'I thought it was just a scratch, Doc,' Neil said, 'one of the perils of the trade, but Dr Alex's been telling me that small scratches from bits of metal, or infected earth, can cause big trouble.'

A fact that Neil knew only too well, Hugh thought, his brows lowering still further, because he'd had a talk with him about it less than a year ago.

'Anyone who works near soil, or with machinery, really must keep their tetanus protection up to date,' Alex said firmly. 'The *Clostridium tetani* bacterium is one of life's nasties, and if you get that in a wound...'

'Neurotoxins can attack the nervous system giving you an abnormal heart rate, difficulty in swallowing and breathing, and jaw rigidity.' Neil shook his head. 'I have to say your bedside manner leaves a lot to be desired, Dr Alex.'

'Just as long as it's sunk in.' She laughed, and Neil did, too, and it was only with the greatest difficulty that Hugh managed to smile as well.

'You want to see me again in a week, Doc?' Neil said, and Alex nodded.

'The antibiotics I gave you should clear the infection,' she replied, 'but your foot's so badly inflamed you might need another course. I also want you to try to keep off your foot as much as possible. I know—I know,' she added as Neil rolled his eyes, 'but will you at least try to delegate some of your work to your men?'

'I'll try,' Neil replied with a grin, and with the briefest of brief nods at Hugh he limped out of the surgery.

'His foot's in a real mess,' Alex said as she handed Neil's folder to Chrissie. 'In fact, if he'd waited a couple more days I'd say we'd have been looking at a case of septicaemia.'

Yeah, well, that was Neil Allen for you, Hugh thought sourly. Big on charm and looks, but not overly big on brains, but the minute he thought that he felt guilty. OK, so the garage owner had been stupid, but he was obviously in great pain and it was crazy of him to feel irritated by his behaviour.

Jealous, more like, his mind whispered, and he stamped on the thought immediately. Of course he wasn't jealous. That was a ridiculous suggestion. It was just that, having appointed himself Alex's minder, he would hardly be much of a protector if he allowed her to get involved with a heartbreaker like Neil Allen.

And you think Alex can't handle someone like Neil Allen? his mind mocked as he saw her smile at something Chrissie had said. Of course she could, but she had also clearly been very badly hurt by her fiancé and she didn't deserve to be hurt again. She was a girl who had been born to laugh, not to cry, and when he thought of her crying…

Unconsciously his fingers clenched. She'd said her engagement had ended after she'd found out something which could only mean she'd discovered Jonathan had been cheating on her, but what kind of scumbag would cheat on a woman like Alex? She was kind, and funny, and feisty, and the more he got to know her the more he could see that although her can-do attitude was a part of her, she was also using it as a shield. A shield to keep other people at bay, and she needed to lower that shield, to let go of the past. But not with someone like Neil Allen.

'Can we make the post-surgery debriefing fast this morning?' Alex said as Chrissie had hurried away to answer the phone. 'I've lots of home visits and, as it's my first slimming and exercise class tonight, I don't want to be late.'

'Not a problem,' Hugh said, leading the way into his consulting room. 'Any concerns about the patients you saw this morning?'

'Only one,' Alex said as she put her medical bag down on

his desk and pulled over a chair. 'Rory Murray's requested a repeat prescription for paracetamol, and that's the second prescription he's had since I diagnosed his osteoarthritis.'

Hugh frowned. 'Not good. I don't want him popping paracetamol like there's no tomorrow. Have you prescribed anti-inflammatory drugs for him instead?'

She shook her head. 'I wanted to check with you first. Taking too many anti-inflammatory drugs is just as bad as taking too much paracetamol. I've asked him to come back tomorrow, and he said, yes, so…'

'You'd like me to see him?'

'I think it might be better as you're going to be in charge of his long-term care.'

After I leave. She hadn't said the words, but that's what she'd meant, and he suddenly realised that he'd actually forgotten about her leaving. Somehow she had managed to slot herself so effortlessly into the practice, become so quickly a part of it, that he'd forgotten she would be leaving.

She doesn't have to go, a small voice pointed out. You could offer her a permanent post. Malcolm would be happy, the patients would be happy, and you…

How often had he heard himself say to Malcolm, 'We'll need to check that with Alex.'? How often had he found himself waiting for the sound of her motorbike when she was out on home visits, always giving a sigh of relief when he saw she was safely back especially now that it was becoming dark so fast? She'd become a good friend in the short time she'd been here, and if she left…He would miss her. It amazed him to have to admit that, after he'd been so unwelcoming to her when she'd first arrived, but he would.

'Alex—'

'I saw Donna in the waiting room,' she interrupted, 'and I have to say she looked downright miserable.'

'She feels it, too.' Hugh sighed. 'Her sugar level is still a little on the high side, and now she's getting stomach cramps.'

'Maybe she's simply not been on the diet long enough,' Alex said, 'or maybe changing her diet isn't enough. She might need hypoglycaemic tablets as well to stimulate her pancreas to produce more insulin.'

'I was wondering whether she might have hypothyroidism instead of Type II diabetes?' he said, and Alex's forehead wrinkled in thought.

'That would certainly explain the muscle weakness, and the stomach cramps, but her heart rate wasn't slow when I sounded her. Has she noticed her skin becoming very dry and flaky, maybe her hair getting thinner, or her voice sounding slightly deeper?'

'No, no, and no,' Hugh admitted. 'I've taken more blood and urine samples, and asked the lab to check her level of thyroid hormones, but it's a puzzle, Alex, and I don't like puzzles.'

'Neither do I,' Alex said, 'but I've got to admit I'm stumped unless she has both Type II diabetes *and* hypothyroidism, which is possible.'

'Yes, but…'

'You still think it's something else.' Alex nodded. 'I don't suppose we could simply pack her off to the hospital, and ask them to test her for everything?'

'I can just imagine the kind of letter I'd get back from the admin department if I tried that.' Hugh laughed.

'So can I,' Alex said, reaching for her bag, but before she could stand up, Chrissie appeared.

'Sorry to interrupt you both,' the receptionist declared, 'but you've another call to add to your home visits, Alex.'

'Not a problem,' Alex replied, and Chrissie grinned.

'I wouldn't be too sure about that. It's Lady Soutar.'

'*The* Lady Soutar?' Alex said, and Hugh rolled his eyes.

'There is only one,' he said. 'Thank God.'

'OK, give,' Alex demanded, when Chrissie had gone. 'What's so very awful about Lady Soutar?'

Hugh's expression became wry.

'Lady Beatrice Soutar is a widow, aged sixty-something, but you'd have to put lighted matches under her fingernails to find out how much older than sixty. Her husband's family have owned Glen Dhu lodge for the past hundred years, and she has two sons, both married, and both terrified witless of her even though they're now in their forties.'

'A formidable lady, in other words,' Alex observed.

'And then some.' Hugh nodded. 'She spends six months of the year at Glen Dhu, and the rest of the year at her house in London which is pretty unusual. Most of the landowners around here come and stay for a month, if we're lucky.'

There was an uncharacteristic note of bitterness in his voice, and Alex's eyebrows rose.

'I didn't realise you disliked landowners so much.'

'I don't dislike them per se,' he replied, 'but too many of them bring nothing to the area. Too many think that if they can afford to buy a Highland estate it also gives them the right to treat the place like one gigantic playground.'

'Hey, I'm neither rich, nor a landowner, remember?' Alex said, and Hugh shook his head ruefully.

'Sorry, but absentee landlords are one of the things I feel very passionate about. Nobody should have the power to decide whether whole families are happy or miserable.'

'I can't bear injustice either,' she said, seeing the anger in his eyes. 'Jonathan…my fiancé…He used to say I should have been called Jude—after the patron saint of lost causes. "Stick to medicine," he used to say. "It's what you're paid for."'

'He definitely wasn't the right man for you,' Hugh observed, and she smiled faintly.

'I guess not, but your antagonism towards landowners—it's personal for you, isn't it? It's not just the politics of the situation, or a feeling of sympathy for those involved, it's personal.'

He smiled. 'How very acute of you. Yes, it's personal. My forebears came from this area originally, you see. They were dirt-poor crofters, forced to scrape a living out of land no one could ever make a living out of, until they were thrown out of their homes to make way for sheep.'

'What happened to them?' she asked, and saw the anger come back into his eyes.

'Some emigrated to the US, and made good, but most—like my great-grandparents—ended up in the slums of Glasgow. They worked every hour God sent to give their son—my grandfather—a better life, just as he did for my father, and my father did for me.'

'Which is why you came back here,' she said slowly. 'You wanted to put two fingers to your nose at the landowners, to show them you'd succeeded, and you also wanted to make them see you had a right to be here.'

'It was partly that,' he admitted, 'but it was also—and I know this is going to sound very pretentious—I came back because I thought—I hoped—my presence might make a difference, that I might be able to ensure that everyone—whether they were rich or poor—got the best possible medical care.'

'I don't think that sounds pretentious at all,' she said. 'I think it's a wonderful aim.'

'And you've done it again, haven't you?' he said wryly. 'Managed to get me talking about myself. Malcolm said I needed to talk to somebody—either a counsellor, or someone I could trust—and it looks like I decided to choose someone I could trust.'

'You trust me?' she said, completely taken aback.

'You're a good person, Alex Lorimer.'

Her throat closed.

'Hugh, I…I'm not the person you seem to think I am,' she managed to say. 'I've made mistakes in the past, done things I wish I hadn't.'

'Haven't we all?' he protested. 'And I didn't say you were perfect. I said you were a good person. You can also be bloody minded, cussed, opinionated—'

'*Hey*,' she protested, relieved to be able to take refuge in outrage, even if her outrage was faked. 'You've just told me you're a real Highland highlander. What happened to the traditional manners and courtesy?'

He grinned. 'I'm one of the black sheep highlanders who tells it like it is and, before you ask, it would take a knife at my throat to get me into a kilt. My bony knees are not for public consumption.'

She'd bet money he didn't have bony knees. She'd bet even more money that he would look absolutely stunning in a kilt. He was so tall for a start, with such very broad shoulders, and with those grey eyes and his thick black hair, she just knew he would look handsome, and sexy, and utterly and completely desirable.

Oh, wake up and face reality, Alex, she told herself as she stared at him. This man doesn't even realise you're a woman. You're just ever-smiling, always-joking Alex, and you should be relieved that's how he sees you, because if he ever did realise you're a woman…

'Alex?'

Hugh's expression was curious, and she forced a smile to her lips.

'I'm sorry,' she said. 'What were we talking about?'

His grey eyes gleamed. 'My bony knees.'

'No, we weren't,' she said determinedly. 'You were telling me about Lady Soutar, and how much you dislike her.'

'I don't dislike her,' he replied. 'As landowners go, she's one of the good ones. She takes care of her tenants' properties, doesn't overfish the river, and keeps her deer under control. The trouble is we strongly suspect she has a gastric ulcer. She, unfortunately,' he continued with a wry smile, 'has decided she's simply suffering from indigestion, and whenever she has a bad bout she calls one of us out, we tell her she has an ulcer, she calls us quacks, forces an antacid prescription out of us, then sends us on our way with a flea in our ear.'

Alex frowned. 'And this happens how often?'

'Generally after she's held a big dinner party, and as she holds rather a lot of dinner parties during the season and the parties go on until quite late...'

'You often get called out in the middle of the night,' Alex finished for him. 'Anything else I should know about her?'

'She's a real stickler for protocol. Don't ever call her Beatrice or she'll poleaxe you.' A slight frown pleated his forehead as he stared at her leathers. 'Look, perhaps I should take the call. Lady Soutar's not for the faint-hearted.'

'Hey, I'm the woman who recklessly throws herself out of planes, and down rapids, remember?' Alex declared. 'I can handle it.'

She reached to retrieve her medical bag, and Hugh put out his hand to stay her.

'Alex, you do know if there's something wrong—if you have a problem—a worry—you can talk to me?'

She gazed at him with dismay. He wasn't talking about Lady Soutar, she knew he wasn't, just as she also knew there was no point in pretending to misunderstand him—he was far too shrewd for that.

'There's nothing wrong,' she said, all chirpily upbeat. *Please, don't have guessed I'm finding you more and more*

attractive with every passing day. Please don't have guessed.
'I can't imagine why you should think I have a problem.'

'I just thought…' He shrugged awkwardly. 'You've seemed a bit down, and a little distracted, this week.'

'I'm fine,' she insisted. 'Just a little tired, that's all.'

'Alex.' He opened his mouth, then paused, clearly trying to decide how best to say what he wanted to say. 'Asking for—and accepting—help isn't a sign of weakness. When Jenny died, I pushed Chrissie and Malcolm away, refused to let them help me, and I know now that I shouldn't have.'

'They're obviously very good friends,' she replied, 'but I prefer to take care of myself. That way I won't ever be disappointed or let down.'

'It can also be a very lonely way to live,' he said gently. 'I know. I've done it.'

Yes, but the people who loved you wanted to help, she thought. The person I loved didn't.

'Hugh, I am *fine*—honestly I am,' she said, and he shook his head at her.

'I don't think you are, and if you should ever change your mind, want a friendly ear…'

'You'll be the first to know,' she said, picking up her bag. 'And now I really *do* have to go. I'll leave seeing Lady Soutar until I've completed all of my other home visits—'

'I think I should come with you,' he interrupted. 'Alex, she doesn't know you,' he continued, as she gazed heavenwards with exasperation, 'and if you just roar up there unannounced she might not be particularly pleased, whereas if I drive along behind you, introduce you when we get there…'

'You're fussing over me again, aren't you?' she exclaimed. 'Hugh, I'm thirty years old. I outgrew the need for a nanny a long time ago.'

'I know,' he said with great and obvious patience, 'but I

don't think anyone ever outgrows the need for a friend, and that's what I hope I am, Alex. A friend.'

He meant it, she knew he did, and she'd never had a man offer to be her friend before. Her lover, yes, but never her friend, and stupidly—crazily—she knew that if he said much more she was going to burst into tears.

'I hope we're friends, too,' she said through a throat so tight it hurt.

'So, do I get to come to Lady Soutar with you?' he pressed, and she managed a shaky chuckle.

'OK—all right—you can come,' she said. 'I'll do my other morning visits first, then I'll telephone you, and you can meet me at Glen Dhu, but once you've introduced me you disappear.'

'Alex—'

'You promise you'll disappear, Hugh, or I won't phone you.'

He sighed. 'I'll disappear,' he said.

'Wow,' Alex gasped as she gazed up at the castellated turrets of Glen Dhu lodge. 'Wow, wow, and double wow.'

'If you think this is impressive,' Hugh observed, 'wait until you see inside. It's *Brigadoon* gone mad. Tartan carpets, tartan curtains, stuffed deer heads on the walls, not to mention the claymores, pikes and dirks.'

'I'm surprised she doesn't have her own personal piper,' Alex said faintly, and Hugh laughed.

'Actually, she does, but thankfully he only ever plays in the evenings. Nervous?' he added, as he saw Alex look ruefully down at her leathers.

Her chin came up.

'Nerves of steel, me,' she replied.

She was going to need them, Hugh thought, as Lady Soutar appeared at Glen Dhu's large oak door, resplendent in a tartan skirt and matching jacket, her steel-grey hair tightly curled and a very definite frown on her face.

'And you are?' Lady Soutar demanded as she came down the steps to meet them, her eyes fixed on Alex.

'Lady Soutar,' Hugh began, 'this is—'

'I didn't ask you, Dr Scott,' she interrupted. 'I was speaking to this young woman.'

'I'm Dr Lorimer, Lady Soutar,' Alex said quickly, seeing Hugh's *I-told-you-so* look. 'The new locum. You asked for a home visit—'

'And you're doing them in packs now, are you?' Lady Soutar exclaimed. 'Sounds to me like your surgery doesn't have enough to do.'

'Dr Scott was simply showing me how to get here,' Alex said. 'He's just leaving.'

'Stay,' Lady Soutar declared imperiously, as Hugh turned to go. 'John will show you through to the kitchen and cook will make you some coffee while this young lady makes me out a prescription for antacid.'

'That's most kind of you, Lady Soutar,' Hugh replied, seeing the long-suffering look on the face of the manservant who had appeared at the top of the steps, 'but I really don't have time—'

'If you have time to show this young lady out here, you have time for a coffee,' Lady Soutar announced. 'As for you, young woman, come along. I don't have all day even if you have.'

'Right.' Alex nodded, and, with a *what-have-you-got-me-into* look at Hugh, she followed Lady Soutar into the house, leaving Hugh with nothing to do but follow John.

'I'd drink your coffee fast, if I were you, Dr Scott,' the man-servant observed. 'Her ladyship's not in a very good mood this afternoon, what with her indigestion, and judging by the looks she was giving the young lady's leather outfit I'd say Dr Lorimer has twenty-five minutes tops before she'll be leaving us.'

That would have been Hugh's estimate, too, but when he went through to the drawing room after having drunk his coffee there was no sign of Alex, or of Lady Soutar. He could, however, hear the distant sound of voices outside, and groaned inwardly. Things must have gone really badly if Lady Soutar was escorting Alex off the premises, but when he hurried out of the front door the sight that greeted him stopped him dead in his tracks. Lady Soutar was laughing at something Alex had said, and Alex was beaming back.

'Glad to see you've finally employed somebody who knows her arse from her elbow, Dr Scott,' Lady Soutar declared when she caught sight of him. 'Alex, dear, how long do you think it will take for that appointment at the hospital to be finalised?'

'It shouldn't take long, Bunty,' Alex replied. 'I'm hoping no longer than a couple of weeks.'

'Good—good,' Lady Soutar said, and with a brief nod at Hugh she went back up the steps of her home and disappeared inside, and Hugh turned slowly to Alex.

'*Bunty?*' he said faintly.

'She asked me to call her that,' Alex declared, 'and even better she's agreed to go to the hospital for tests. She's a real sweetie, Hugh.'

'She's a…' Hugh shook his head. 'How did you do that— *how*? She has been putting Malcolm and me through hell for the last ten years and you come along on one visit and suddenly she can't wait to go to the hospital.'

'Well, she was a bit frosty at first, but I think that's just her way,' Alex replied. 'I noticed, however, that she kept glancing out of the window at my bike so I asked her if she was interested in bikes.'

'And?'

'It turns out that Bunty's father made his fortune in manu-facturing, but what he really wanted was to race motorcycles so he used to take Bunty and her brothers all over the world to watch the big races, and she got hooked, too. She wanted to know all about my Ducati. How long I'd had it, how fast it went, when I'd started riding. Would you believe, she was the same age as me when she got her first bike?'

'I'd believe anything at the moment,' Hugh said with feeling. 'Alex, if I was wearing a hat, I'd take it off to you. You're a miracle worker.'

In more ways than one, he decided as he drove back to Kilbreckan, with Alex following close behind, and his jaw dropped when he saw all the cars packed into the car park outside the surgery, and the number of excited, chattering women who had clearly turned up for Alex's class. Jenny had been lucky if eight women turned up to her class whereas it looked as though every overweight woman in Kilbreckan had arrived for Alex's.

'I don't know how we're going to fit everybody into the waiting room,' Chrissie said, looking distinctly harassed as she pushed her way through the throng. 'Malcolm's taken out all the chairs, but even so—'

'He's back from the seminar?' Hugh interrupted, then frowned when he saw his partner coming out of their small office. 'Played hookey for the last session, did you?'

'You bet I did,' Malcolm replied. 'It was the same old, same old, and I had no intention of missing the first of Alex's classes.'

'You just want to make fun of us,' Chrissie protested. 'Alex, tell Hugh and Malcolm they're banned from watching,' she continued as Alex stowed her helmet under the reception desk.

'No can do, I'm afraid,' Alex replied. 'They want to satisfy themselves that I'm not doing anything which will put the entire female population of Kilbreckan into traction, but don't worry. If they cause any sort of trouble, I'll get Mrs Allen to eject them. Give me ten minutes to change into my costume and I'll be right with you.'

Malcolm gulped as Alex disappeared and Chrissie began ushering the women through to the room normally used by their visiting physiotherapist.

'By costume, you don't think Alex means the full…you know…' Malcolm gestured awkwardly towards his chest and his legs. 'That sort of costume?'

'Even if she does,' Hugh said firmly, 'I'm sure we've both seen a lot more feminine skin when we've been down at the beach in the summer.'

'Not on Kilbreckan beach, we haven't,' Malcolm muttered. 'Most women wear thermals on Kilbreckan beach in the summer if they don't want to catch pneumonia.'

'Malcolm, we're doctors,' Hugh protested. 'We see women's bodies every day of our working lives.'

But not like this, he thought, as Alex reappeared, and his mouth went suddenly dry. No woman had ever come into his surgery wearing a green sequinned bra that fitted a pair of small yet surprisingly full breasts like a second skin. No woman had ever stood before him clad in a green and gold, floor-length skirt, split almost to her waist, that sat tantalisingly low on her hips, revealing a flawlessly smooth stomach, and a pair of surprisingly long legs.

'Alex, you look lovely,' Malcolm said, admiration plain in his voice. 'Just like a woman. I mean, I know you're a woman,' he added quickly, crimsoning slightly, 'but usually…I mean, at work…that's to say…'

'It's all right, Malcolm.' She laughed as his cheeks began to resemble those of a ripe tomato. 'I know what you mean.'

'She does look lovely, doesn't she, Hugh?' Malcolm continued, giving him a pointed look, and Hugh cleared his throat.

He'd called her a pixie, a water sprite, because she was so small and willowy, but the woman standing in front of him was also unmistakably—indisputably—a woman. A woman with slender hips and shapely thighs. A woman with a woman's breasts and, as he found his eyes travelling down to them, he jerked them back her face, and kept them there.

'She…' He cleared his throat again. 'She looks very nice.'

Stunning would have been more accurate, he thought, and for a split second he thought he saw hurt and disappointment in her eyes but, before he could rectify what he'd said, be more complimentary, she'd turned to face the assembled women.

'OK, let's get this class started,' she said.

'Alex, it doesn't need both Malcolm and me to assess the safety risks of your class,' Hugh said quickly, but before he could retreat she put out a hand to stop him.

'Stay right where you are, Hugh Scott,' she exclaimed. 'No way are you going to weasel out of watching after all the fuss you made about it not being safe. You're going to stay, and eat your words.'

He didn't want to stay. He didn't want to be anywhere near her at all, not when he couldn't keep his eyes off her, but she'd already closed the door, and was explaining to the women that the first step they were going to learn was something called the Egyptian Walk.

A walk that was clearly extremely difficult if the lack of success being displayed was anything to go by when Alex switched on her cassette, and a rhythmic tune began to play, and the women in the room attempted to copy what she was doing.

'Are they all supposed to look like drunken sailors leaving the pub at closing time?' Malcolm muttered, his teeth sunk deep into his bottom lip to keep himself from laughing out loud, but Alex heard him.

'Dr Scott—Dr MacIntyre!' she exclaimed, fixing them

both with her green eyes. 'You're not wearing scarves round your hips.'

'Alex—belly dancing—it's a woman's thing,' Hugh protested, and she shook her head.

'No, it's not. It's become a female dance because of its links with mother nature and fertility, but in the past young men used to belly dance.'

'Come on, Dr Scott,' Mrs Allen shouted. 'You're always telling us how beneficial exercise is, let's see how fit you are.'

'No—really—perhaps some other time,' Hugh began, holding up his hands in apology. 'I'm just an observer this evening.'

'Thirty-nine going on sixty, Hugh,' Alex said as she bore down on him with a scarf in her hand and a look on her face that told him she wouldn't take no for an answer.

Out of the corner of his eye he could see Chrissie tying a scarf round Malcolm's ample hips despite his protestations. Short of making a run for the door—a run Hugh strongly suspected that Mrs Allen with her considerable girth and experience of raising eight sons would assuredly forestall—there was nothing he could do but give in with as much grace as he could.

'I look stupid,' he muttered as Alex wrapped a scarf round his hips.

'And that matters?' she said, her voice uncharacteristically brittle, and before he could reply she'd returned to the front of the class, leaving him feeling like a prize idiot with nowhere to hide.

He felt even more stupid as the class progressed because no matter how hard he tried he just couldn't get the steps right. It was so much more difficult than it looked, and he had to acknowledge that Alex had been right when she'd said belly dancing was good exercise. All around him he could see faces screwed up in concentration as the women tried to mimic what Alex was doing, faces that became redder and redder as Alex demonstrated more and more difficult moves, and he could feel a trickle of sweat running down his own back.

'OK, I think that's enough for this evening,' Alex declared after an hour. 'Same time next week, ladies?'

A chorus of ready assent went up, and Hugh let out a sigh of relief that it was over until Ellie Dickson put up her hand.

'Could you show us what a complete dance looks like, Dr Alex?' she said. 'So we know what can be achieved after a few more exercises?'

'Yes, go on, please,' the rest of the women entreated, and Alex smiled.

'OK. I'll do a short dance for you, incorporating as many of the moves as I can, and then finish up with what's called a shimmy, but I don't want any of you to try this at home. You'll all need quite a few more lessons before you're supple enough.'

Hugh didn't know what a shimmy was, and neither could he have identified any of the steps Alex incorporated into her dance, but he did know when she began to dance that what she was able to do was pretty special.

Who would have thought, he wondered, as he stared at her whirling, undulating body, that a pair of jeans and a sweatshirt, or a pair of leathers, hid a body that was capable of performing such intricate and complicated moves? But, as he continued to watch, and Alex danced faster and faster, dipping and twirling and spinning, he suddenly realised something else.

That the libido he'd believed long dead had suddenly and very painfully come alive. That his body was stirring and hardening as he stared at her, and he wanted to reach out and caress the breasts she was somehow making quiver and tremble to the music. He wanted to bury himself between the smooth pale thighs that glistened and gleamed with the effort of the dance, and he was appalled.

'You OK, buddy?' Malcolm said curiously when Alex's dance had ended, and the assembled women began to clap and cheer, and Hugh pulled the scarf off his hips and crumpled it into a tight ball in his fist.

He could see Alex staring at him from across the room, her face flushed, her breasts rising and falling rapidly from her exertions, her expression a little uncertain, a little hesitant, almost shy. She was waiting for him to compliment her on her dance, he knew she was, but he had to get away, just had to. Blindly he turned on his heel, but he got not further than the car park before he heard her calling his name, and, unwillingly, he turned to face her.

Her crazy red hair was sticking out all over the place from her exertions, but what he was most aware of was how very large her eyes were in the moonlight, and how lost she suddenly looked. A lost water sprite with lips that looked soft, oh, so soft, and as he stared down at her he felt his heart lurch against his rib cage, heard a rushing in his ears, and he wanted to kiss her, so very much wanted to kiss her, and it was *wrong*.

'Hugh, what is it?' she said, her face no longer flushed but pale. 'What's the matter?'

'Alex…'

He took a step towards her, but women were beginning to stream out of the surgery, chattering and laughing, and unconsciously he shook his head, and Alex half stretched out her hand to him, and then Grace Allen was beside her, talking animatedly, and he headed for his car, not looking back, not trusting himself to look back.

No, his brain declared emphatically, as he drove home, scarcely seeing the road. *No*, it repeated, when he opened his front door and strode into his sitting room. What he had felt when he'd watched Alex dance was a betrayal of Jenny's memory. A betrayal of all that had been good and pure and decent between them.

He pulled files out of his bag, and tried to concentrate on them but it didn't work. He switched on the television and tried to lose himself in the documentary that was showing, but that didn't work either. All he kept seeing was Alex, with her green eyes shining. Alex's lithe stomach undulating, and her breasts straining against the fine fabric of her bra.

Desperately, he took the photograph of Jenny from his wallet and stared down at her familiar smiling face. This was real, he told himself, not what he had felt this evening for Alex, this was real, but, as he continued to gaze at the photograph it wasn't Jenny's face he saw, it was Alex standing in the car park, Alex looking so lost, so very lost and alone.

A sob broke from him, and he put his fist to his mouth to quell the others he knew would come, and then from a great distance, he suddenly heard his wife's voice.

'Let me go, Hugh,' she whispered. 'It's time for you to let me go.'

He had loved Jenny so much but she was right. She wouldn't have wanted him to spend the rest of his life grieving for her. She would have wanted him to go on, to keep living, and he hadn't been living since she died, only existing, and with an effort he put Jenny's photograph back into his wallet, then stumbled to his bed, and eventually fell asleep. But for the first time in two years he didn't dream of Jenny.

He dreamt of Alex.

CHAPTER FIVE

'HUGH and Malcolm are both ready for the post-surgery debrief-ing,' Chrissie declared as she opened Alex's consulting-room door. ' Shall I tell them you'll be along, or...?' The reception-ist's gaze fell on the folders lying scattered on Alex's desk. 'Do you need a few more minutes to finish your paperwork?'

'Tell them I'm coming,' Alex replied, hitching a smile to her lips, but she groaned when the receptionist disappeared.

She hadn't even started her paperwork. For the past hour she'd done nothing but stare into space, and doodle on her notebook, and what had she drawn? Boxes. Dozens and dozens of boxes.

'Freudian, or what, Alex?' she muttered, quickly tearing the top sheet out of her notebook, and tossing it into her waste-paper basket, but it didn't help.

She could still see the boxes and herself trapped inside them.

Savagely she bit her lip. She should never have worn her belly dancing costume that night. She hadn't needed to, not for the first lesson, and certainly not when she'd known Hugh was going to be there, but when she'd got back to Kilbreckan that night, after meeting Bunty Soutar, some malignant demon had whispered, *Put your costume on, put it on,* and what had been the result?

'You look nice,' Hugh had said when he'd first seen her.

She'd been so disappointed, so hurt, and when she'd danced for him—and she *had* danced for him, she knew she had—he'd walked away from her, not once but twice, but since then...

Everywhere she went in the surgery he seemed to be there, hovering. Every time she looked up at post-practice meetings, his eyes were on her, thoughtful, pensive, and yet also with something else that made her heart skitter and her pulses race.

But that's what you wanted, her mind pointed out. *That's why you put on the costume, because you wanted him to realise that you're a woman, and now he obviously has, what's the problem?*

I don't want to hurt him, her heart cried, and I know I will. I don't want to be hurt again myself, and I know I will. I should have thought it through, stayed in my sweatshirt and jeans, remained good old sexless Alex, but I didn't, and I was wrong.

'Sorry, Alex, memory like a sieve this morning,' Chrissie declared apologetically as she reappeared at Alex's consulting-room door. 'Hugh says he'd like a word with you after the meeting if that's OK with you?'

'Absolutely. Not a problem, ' Alex replied, all chirpily upbeat but when Chrissie disappeared again she groaned again as she got wearily to her feet. 'You shouldn't have been drawing boxes, Alex Lorimer,' she told the empty room. 'You should have been drawing straitjackets, because that's where you belong.'

'Lady Soutar has an appointment at the hospital next week with Mr Denara for her upper gastrointestinal endoscopy,' Hugh observed, holding out the letter to Alex.

'Terrific,' she replied, scanning the letter quickly, then passing it across to Malcolm. 'Hopefully this will soon mean an end to all her midnight calls.'

'Always providing she actually turns up for the endoscopy,' Malcolm declared, and Alex shook her head.

'She'll go,' she said with conviction. 'Bunty's a woman of her word, and she gave me her word, so she'll go. What do we know about the consultant, Mr Denara?'

'He's good,' Malcolm replied. 'One of the old-school, no-nonsense types.'

'Which is just as well otherwise Bunty would make mincemeat of him.' Hugh laughed.

'Look, just because she can be a bit overbearing at times, doesn't mean it's wrong for her to have a mind of her own,' Alex said with considerably more edge than she'd intended. 'She's a widow, she's had to take care of herself for the past twenty years. OK, she has two sons but for all we know they might be completely useless, and that's why she's had to become strong, because the only person she can depend on is herself.'

'Right,' Malcolm murmured, and, as Alex took an uneven breath and stared down at her notebook, she didn't see the big man raise his eyebrows at Hugh, and Hugh shake his head back, clearly equally puzzled.

'Donna Ferguson's blood samples confirm she definitely has an underactive thyroid,' Hugh declared, 'but her sugar levels are still too high which would also suggest she has Type II diabetes.'

'She could be suffering from both hypothyroidism *and* Type II diabetes,' Malcolm pointed out. 'It's not unusual in women of Donna's age.'

'I know, but I just can't help thinking…' Hugh shook his head. 'Oh, hell, I don't know what I'm thinking, except I can't get rid of the feeling that there's something I'm missing. What do you think, Alex?'

'I'm a great believer in gut feeling,' she said. 'If you're unhappy, then I'd say keep digging.'

'Yes, but all these tests I keep giving her,' Hugh declared. 'Donna's starting to lose confidence in me, and that's not good in any patient/doctor relationship.'

He was right, it wasn't, and somewhere in the back of Alex's mind a faint memory stirred, of something she had read years ago in a medical book.

'Is it worth asking the hospital to perform a serum transferrin saturation test on the blood samples you took?' she said.

'You think she could have haemochromatosis—too much iron in her blood?' Malcolm said.

'I don't know,' Alex admitted, 'but labs don't automatically measure the amount of iron bound to the transferrin protein, do they? You have to specifically ask them to check it out.'

Hugh's forehead pleated. 'Haemochromatosis is normally an inherited disease, Alex, and her father is a very hale and hearty ninety-year-old.'

'But her mother is dead, and so is her sister,' Alex said. 'Yes, I know, I know,' she continued, holding up her hand as he tried to interrupt, 'they both died of breast cancer but haemochromatosis doesn't usually manifest itself in women until they reach the menopause, so…'

'You think that as neither of them lived long enough to reach the menopause, perhaps neither of them lived long enough to develop the disease?' Hugh's frown deepened. 'It would certainly explain her aching joints, high blood sugar levels and underactive thyroid, but…'

'I'd say go for it,' Malcolm declared. 'OK, so it's yet another test, but what have we to lose?'

'Unanimous decision?' Hugh said, glancing from Malcolm

to Alex, and when they both nodded, he smiled. 'OK, we'll ask the hospital to test her for haemochromatosis, and if you're right, Alex, I owe you one.'

'And she'll collect, believe me.' Malcolm laughed, and Hugh laughed, but Alex barely managed a smile.

Instead, she stared back down at her notebook, and Malcolm frowned questioningly at Hugh again, and Hugh jerked his head meaningfully towards the door.

'Right,' Malcolm said, getting briskly to his feet. 'I'd better be off. It's my weekly visit to the old folks' home, and I don't want to miss their morning coffee. Sister Mackay makes the best scones in the north.'

'I'd better hit the road, too,' Alex said, getting to her feet, but Hugh held up his hand to stop her.

'Didn't Chrissie tell you I'd like a word?' he said.

Yes, but I was hoping you might have forgotten, she thought, as Malcolm hurried away and she gazed enviously after him. I was praying you might have forgotten, but he obviously hadn't, and reluctantly she sat down again.

'So, what did you want to talk to me about?' she said when she and Hugh were alone.

'Malcolm and I want to offer you a permanent post with us in our practice.'

Whatever else she had been expecting him to say, it hadn't been that, and as he smiled at her, clearly expecting her to accept, her heart slid slowly down to the foot of her stomach. It had been so easy to refuse the offer of a permanent post from the other GPs she had worked with, but this was going to be harder, so much harder.

Then tell him you'll stay, her mind whispered, but she couldn't do that, she knew she couldn't, not when she was so attracted to him, not when he said he trusted her, and she hadn't told him the truth about herself.

'Hugh, I…' She came to a halt, cleared her throat and began again. 'I'm very flattered that you and Malcolm would like me to join you here, but I'm afraid I can't accept your offer. I've agreed to help out at a practice in Cumbria next month, then I'm going to Lisbon for a couple of weeks in January, and in February I'll be working in Glasgow.'

The smile that had been on his face when she'd begun speaking had vanished completely by the time she was finished, and in its place was confusion and bewilderment.

'But can't you simply tell the agency you're no longer available for locum work?' he protested. 'That you've accepted a full-time post here? I appreciate you won't want to give up your holiday in Lisbon, but Malcolm and I would be more than happy to cope for those two weeks.'

Oh, please don't make this any more difficult than it already is, she thought, seeing not only confusion but also hurt in his grey eyes. Please, can't you just accept that I can't stay here, that I have to go?

'I'm really sorry,' she said. *And I am, I am.* 'But I can't accept your offer.'

'But why?' he demanded. 'You fit in here so well, and you like it here, I know you do. If it's your New Year challenges that are bothering you, I'm sure we can figure something out, perhaps give you a longer annual leave to enable you to undertake them.'

Oh, don't, please *don't*, she thought, feeling a hard lump in her throat. You've no idea of how much I want to say yes, but it wouldn't be fair to you or to Malcolm.

'You have a wonderful practice, Hugh,' she said as evenly as she could, 'but staying here…It's not for me. I'm sorry, but it's not for me.'

'But, Alex—'

She didn't give him time to reply. She just headed out of

his room as fast as she could, and when she shut the door behind her Hugh slumped back in his seat, torn between bafflement and anger.

She hadn't so much as hesitated before she'd refused his offer. She'd just given him a flat, unequivocal no, and it didn't make any sense. She liked the patients, and the patients liked her. She liked Malcolm, and he knew, too, though he wasn't a vain man, that she liked him, so why would she want to leave?

Well, he was damned if he was going to let her go, he decided, at least not without a fight. She had somehow crept into his life—bulldozed into it, more like, he thought ruefully—and he couldn't imagine his life without her, refused point blank to.

'Well?' Malcolm said hopefully as he stuck his head round Hugh's consulting-room door, and Hugh frowned at him.

'I thought you were going to the old folks' home for coffee and scones?' he said, and Malcolm grinned.

'I am, but when you said earlier that you were going to offer Alex a partnership this morning I knew I couldn't leave without finding out what she said.'

'She refused.'

'She refused?' Malcolm repeated, amazement plain on his face, then he sighed. 'Well, that's it, then. You'll want me to phone the agency, to arrange for them to send us another locum.'

'No,' Hugh said grimly, 'because this isn't over yet. There's something she's not telling me, something she's holding back, and I'm not going to rest until I find out what it is.'

A slow smile crept across Malcolm's plump face.

'Like that, is it?' he said, and Hugh's own lips curved ruefully.

'Not yet, but I'd like it to be,' he said. 'I care about her, Malcolm. I care a lot, and there's something wrong here, something she's scared about, and I want to know what it is.'

'Be careful, Hugh.' Malcolm warned. 'You know what Alex is like. If you antagonise her, she'll clam up like a shell.'

'I'll be careful,' Hugh replied.

But not that careful, he thought as he buried himself in the practice paperwork for the rest of the day. He wanted answers, and not just answers. He also wanted to tell her that no matter what Jonathan had done, she had to let go of the past because if she didn't it was just going to fester, as his own grief and guilt had festered.

This evening, he told himself. There was no surgery this evening, so he'd corner her when she got back from her home visits, and he wouldn't let her leave the surgery until she'd listened to him.

But it looked as though he was going to have a long wait, he realised, when he carried all the folders he'd been working on through to Chrissie's small office and saw it was almost six o'clock.

'Alex, not back yet?' he said as Chrissie shook her head.

'Mr Nolan phoned from Heatherlea farm at three o'clock to say his wife had fallen and he thought she might have broken her leg so I paged the call through to Alex.'

Hugh nodded, but Heatherlea was only a forty-five-minute ride away, and Alex would have been coming back from her home visits by three o'clock so where the hell was she?

'Hugh?'

Chrissie looked uncertain, and a little worried, and he managed a smile.

'You get off home,' he said. 'I'll give Alex another half an hour, then I'll phone the Nolans to see what the problem is.'

He lasted only five minutes in the empty surgery after Chrissie had gone. Five minutes of pacing up and down, picturing Alex lying out on the road somewhere, her bike having hit a deer, her slender body bruised and broken, was enough to have him dialling the Nolans' number, and he didn't know whether to cheer or swear when it wasn't the Nolans who answered, but Alex.

'What the hell's wrong?' he demanded, his worry making him sound angrier and more impatient than he'd intended. 'Why are you still there?'

'There's a problem,' Alex said. 'I'm almost one hundred per cent certain Mrs Nolan hasn't broken her leg, just very badly jarred and bruised it, but I want her to go to hospital to have it X-rayed, and she's refusing to go.'

Hugh frowned at the phone. Alex sounded unsure, upset, and completely unlike herself.

'I'm on way,' he said.

'There's no need,' Alex began. 'I can—'

'I'm on my way,' he said, and put down the phone before she could protest any further.

'If you've come here as backup for your partner,' Frank Nolan said the minute he opened his front door and saw Hugh standing there, 'you've wasted your time. You can't make my wife go into hospital if she doesn't want to.'

'No, I can't,' Hugh said mildly, stepping forward so Frank Nolan had no other option but to let him in, 'but the fact that you actually phoned my practice, asking for a doctor, suggests you're worried about your wife.'

'Of course I'm worried,' Frank Nolan exclaimed. 'She's my wife, and I love her, but she doesn't want to go to hospital.'

'And, as I keep telling Mr Nolan,' Alex declared appearing behind him, 'although I don't think his wife's leg is broken, I really would be happier if the X-ray department verified it.'

A faint feminine voice called from somewhere in the house, and, as Frank Nolan headed off instantly towards it, Hugh looked at Alex, his eyebrows raised.

'OK, what's going on here?'

'Irene Nolan has multiple sclerosis,' Alex replied wearily. 'That's why she has so many bruises—she keeps falling over—but she and her husband have decided they want to go down the holistic path with her treatment.'

'But you can't holistically treat a broken leg,' Hugh protested.

'And you think I don't know that?' Alex exclaimed. 'I've gone over and over the same ground with them for the past two hours, and they just won't listen. It's…it's…' She sniffed. 'It's like talking to a brick wall.'

It was the sniff that did it. Alex wasn't a sniffing sort of a woman. Alex was a life-is-there-to-be-grabbed-by-the-throat sort of a girl, and without thinking Hugh put his arm round her.

'Hey, come on,' he said softly. 'It's not like you to get so down.'

'I know.' She sniffed again. 'But Irene and Frank Nolan… They obviously love one another so much, and yet this hospital thing…'

There was something else here, Hugh thought as he stared down at her. It wasn't just Irene's refusal to go to hospital. Something else had got under Alex's skin, and pushed all of her buttons, big time.

'Alex—'

'I'm sorry,' she muttered, pulling a handkerchief out of her pocket and blowing her nose vigorously. 'I can assure you I'm not usually this feeble.'

'I don't think you're feeble at all,' Hugh protested, holding her tighter. 'I think you're just at the end of your tether, and understandably so.'

'You could say that,' she said, then she stepped out from under his arm, leaving him feeling cold without her. 'She's through here, and I hope you have more luck than I've had.'

Hugh hoped he would have, too, as he followed Alex down

a narrow corridor, and into a small sitting room, and saw Mrs Nolan lying on a sofa, her face chalk-white with pain, her husband hovering anxiously beside her.

'Irene—may I call you Irene?' Hugh asked as he crouched down beside her, and Mrs Nolan nodded. 'I'm Dr Scott, and my partner tells me you have multiple sclerosis. When were you diagnosed?'

'Five years ago,' Mrs Nolan replied. 'I went to the doctors because my foot kept feeling numb. It was a nuisance, nothing more, but Frank…' She smiled weakly up at her husband. 'He insisted I went.'

'Sensible man,' Hugh observed.

'When the doctors told us what was wrong, that there was no cure…' Frank Nolan bit his lip. 'I wasn't about to give up, accept the diagnosis without a fight. We've seen just about every specialist in the country, including quite a few crackpot ones.'

'Frank can be very determined when he wants to be,' Irene Nolan said with a shaky laugh.

'Of course I'm determined,' her husband exclaimed. 'You're my wife, God dammit, and I love you. Do you know she actually told me to divorce her, Doctor?' he continued with a look of exasperation. 'As though her being ill was going to make me love her any less.'

'You clearly don't understand the full power of love, Irene,' Hugh said with a smile, and looked up to catch Alex's eye, to share his incredulity with her, but she wasn't looking at him.

She was looking at Frank Nolan, and her eyes were full of such heartache, such indescribable pain that he almost went to her, but he couldn't, not when his first priority was their patient.

'What medication are you on, Irene?' he asked, forcing his attention back to her.

'I stopped taking everything the hospital prescribed about two years ago,' she replied. 'None of it seemed to help, and so Frank and I decided to try changing my diet to see if that would make a difference, and it did for a while, but just recently I've started to have trouble seeing.'

'She began bumping into things, falling over,' Frank Nolan declared. 'That was when I wondered whether a move to the country might help, as the air is so much cleaner here than it is in the city.'

'You do know that the chances of you going into remission—of the symptoms lessening, or disappearing completely—for a while are good?' Hugh said gently, and the Nolans nodded.

'It's what we're hoping for, Doctor,' Frank Nolan said. 'I don't know how long Irene and I will have together, but I want that time to be the best it can be.'

Faintly, Hugh thought he heard Alex give a small sob, but he kept his gaze fixed on the Nolans. Whatever was upsetting Alex so much would have to wait.

'I couldn't agree with you more, Mr Nolan,' he said, 'which is why I can't understand why you're both so reluctant to have her leg X-rayed. She'd only be at the hospital for a couple of hours, whether the leg is broken or not.'

'That's what the doctor said when I fell and broke my wrist two years ago,' Irene Nolan replied, 'and yet they kept me in for a month, doing all these tests. Tests that only prove what I know already.'

'We know Irene has MS,' Frank Nolan declared, 'and she was so miserable in hospital, Doctor, so very unhappy, and I don't want her to go through that again.'

'What if I came with you to the hospital?' Hugh said. 'Insisted that Irene was only there for her leg to be X-rayed and plastered if necessary, and then you'd be leaving.'

'You'd do that for us?' Irene Nolan said, amazement plain on her face, and Hugh smiled.

'Consider it done. Alex, would you ring for an ambulance?'

She did, and the ambulance was there within minutes.

'Thank you, Doctor,' Frank Nolan said, gripping Hugh's hand tightly, after the paramedics had carefully carried his wife out to the ambulance. 'I know that sounds completely inadequate, but I won't ever forget this.'

Hugh shook his head and grinned.

'Just get in the ambulance with your wife,' he said, and when Mr Nolan had, and the ambulance drove away, Hugh turned to see Alex standing beside her motorbike. 'You, OK?' he continued.

'Why did you come out here?' she said. 'I'm very glad you did, but why did you come?'

'You sounded upset—in trouble—and you're my friend so of course I came,' he replied.

'Just like that?'

He frowned, and shook his head. 'I'm sorry, I don't under-stand what you mean. Why should it surprise you that I came out to help you?'

Because Jonathan wouldn't have, Alex thought. Miss Fix It. That's what he'd used to call her. Little Miss Fix It, and she'd used to laugh at the nickname, until she'd really needed him, and he hadn't been there.

'Alex?'

Hugh was staring at her with a puzzled frown, and she managed a smile.

'You'd better go. The Nolans need you.'

'Yes, but—'

'Go, Hugh,' she insisted, and for a second he hesitated, then he strode to his car, and Alex didn't even wait for him to drive away.

She just hit her ignition and rode off into the dark, with what Hugh had said to Irene Nolan reverberating around in her brain.

'You don't understand the full power of love,' he'd said.

She couldn't have either, she thought, not if what both Frank Nolan and Hugh Scott had felt for their wives was what love—true love—was really like.

And you never will, her mind whispered, and she bit down hard on her lip to quell the tears she could feel welling in her eyes.

Tears never solved anything. Tears didn't change anything. Get something to eat, Alex, she told herself when she got back to her flat. You'll feel better if you have something to eat, but she was so tired, so bone-wearily tired, that she just curled up on the sofa and when she heard a knock on her door an hour later she knew who it was, and wished he would just go away.

'I'm sorry to disturb you,' Hugh said when she reluctantly opened her door, 'but I wondered if I might have a word?'

'Can't it wait, Hugh?' she protested. 'I'm really tired tonight.'

'I'm afraid it can't,' he declared, his face implacable, and she sighed.

He wasn't going to go away. No matter what she said, she knew he wasn't going to go away, and she led the way into her sitting room with resignation.

'OK,' she said as she turned to face him, 'what's so all-fired important that it can't wait until tomorrow?'

'I thought you might like to know that Irene Nolan hasn't broken her leg,' he said. 'You were right. It's just badly jarred and bruised.'

'I'm pleased to hear that,' she said. 'Irene and Frank must be, too.'

He nodded. 'They've signed on with the practice now, as well, so that means we can keep an eye on them both.'

'Good,' she replied, and began to walk pointedly towards her front door. 'Well, if there's nothing else…'

'There is,' he said, staying exactly where he was in the centre of her sitting room. 'I want to know why you refused my offer of a permanent post.'

'Hugh, we've been through this already,' she protested. 'I've agreed to help out in a practice in Cumbria, and then—'

'Alex, what if I asked you to stay,' he interrupted, 'not for the practice, but for me?'

No, her brain protested as she heard the huskiness in his voice, and felt her own heart contract. I don't want you to be attracted to me. I thought I did, but I was wrong, selfish, because it won't work, it can't.

'Hugh, don't make this even more difficult than it already is,' she began, but it was the wrong thing to say because his eyebrows snapped down immediately.

'If this is a difficult decision for you to make,' he said, 'that would suggest you don't want to make it.'

'Hugh—'

'I want to know what's wrong, Alex,' he interrupted. 'I know you're keeping something from me, and I want to know what it is.'

'I'm not keeping anything from you,' she exclaimed. 'I've agreed to work in Cumbria, and when I get back from the rally in Lisbon—'

'The rally in Lisbon?' he interrupted, then dawning comprehension appeared in his eyes and with it also came complete disbelief. 'Dear, lord, you're going to Lisbon to take part in the Lisbon to Dakar Rally, aren't you? Alex, are you *insane*? People *die* in that race. You'll be riding your bike virtually non-stop for sixteen days over 5,000 miles of some of the roughest terrain in the world.'

'Which is why I'm so looking forward to it,' she said. 'It's the ultimate challenge, Hugh, the opportunity of a lifetime.'

'It's complete insanity,' he protested. 'I know you want to

live life to the full, but it seems to me you're sometimes living life as though you don't care whether you live or die.'

'Hugh—'

'As though you're trying to squeeze a whole lifetime into as short a time as possible because…' He came to a halt, and his eyes shot suddenly to hers. 'Oh, my God,' he whispered, 'that's it, isn't it? That's why you never stay anywhere long, why the Nolans upset you so much, why you set yourself these crazy challenges—'

'My challenges aren't crazy.'

'Because there's something wrong with you, isn't there? Alex, I can find out what's wrong,' he continued when she said nothing. 'I can phone the agency, and ask them to give me your medical history, and they'll have to give it to me, you know they will.'

'That's an invasion of my privacy,' she said in outrage, and he nodded.

'Without question it is, which is why I'd far rather you told me yourself. Alex…' He came forward a step. 'Tell me what's wrong. Please.'

He wouldn't give it up, she knew he wouldn't, and maybe it was time—way past time—for her to tell him so he'd understand, and she walked over to the sofa and sat down.

'I…I didn't know there was anything wrong, not right away,' she murmured. 'I'd just finished my GP training, and that winter I seemed to go down with cold after cold. I'd lost weight, too, but of course I was thrilled about that.' She managed a smile. 'What woman wouldn't be?'

'And?' Hugh pressed, and she took a deep breath.

'It was Jonathan who found the lump under my arm. I didn't want to go to the doctor—it seemed such a waste of time for a tiny painless swelling—but Jonathan insisted. As soon as the doctor examined me, he started asking me all these questions, like was I sweating a lot at night, had my skin become more itchy, were my periods heavier than normal?'

Hugh's face whitened. 'Alex, are you saying what I think you're saying?'

'Oh, come on, Hugh, you're a doctor,' she protested, 'you know what it was. So did I, even though I was just newly qualified.'

'Hodgkin's lymphoma,' he said slowly. 'Cancer of the lymphatic system.' He sat down beside her on the sofa. 'Hell, Alex, you must have been terrified.'

'My mum was. She'd only just started to get over my dad's death, and then I had to hit her with the fact that I had Hodgkin's.'

'You had chemo, and radiation therapy?'

She reached up and ran her fingers through her short red hair. 'You asked me why I got my hair cut. When I started the chemo, it all fell out. My mum…she bought me all these weird and wonderful hats and scarves so I wouldn't feel so bad about being bald, but…' Her lip trembled. 'Crazy, isn't it, that even when there's a very strong possibility you'll die, the one thing that makes you cry is when your hair all falls out.'

'But it grew back,' he said gently, and she nodded.

'It grew back, but I've kept it short since then in case…' She tried to smile and failed. 'I figure, if…if the cancer comes back, then maybe it won't seem quite so awful this time when it all falls out again.'

He reached for her hand, and trapped it between his two large ones.

'Alex, between 75 and 95 out of every 100 people who are diagnosed with early stage 1 or 2 Hodgkin's lymphoma stay in remission.'

'Mine was a stage 3B.'

She watched him regroup quickly.

'OK,' he said, 'even for a stage 3 or a stage 4 Hodgkin's—'

'Between 50 and 70 out of every 100 people can be cured, or at the very least the disease can be kept at bay for years,' she finished for him. 'I know. I'm a doctor, remember, which is why I also know that even if the Hodgkin's doesn't come back, I have an increased risk of developing leukaemia.'

'An increased risk, yes, but that doesn't make it a definite.'

She gave a shaky laugh. 'You're good at this, aren't you? Making the patient feel positive about their prognosis.'

He stared down at her hand between his, then up at her, his face gentle, tender.

'Alex, you're not simply a patient to me,' he said. 'You mean more—so much more. Your fiancé…he must have been shattered.'

'Jonathan…' She closed her eyes, reliving the memory. 'He couldn't bear watching me being sick all the time, knowing that even after all the treatment I might still die, so he…he broke off our engagement.'

'He left you because you were ill?' Hugh said with outrage. 'What kind of low-life scumbag walks out on a woman at a time like that?'

'He wasn't—isn't—a low-life scumbag, Hugh,' she said. 'He's…he's just an ordinary man who was scared witless of what I was going through, and it's not unreasonable to expect the person you love to be around for a while and…and to be able to give you children.' Her fingers jerked convulsively in his. 'I can't, you see. The chemo left me infertile, and Jonathan…he comes from a large family.'

'Well, screw him and his big family,' Hugh exclaimed. 'Alex, you don't ask somebody to marry you because you want children. You ask them to marry you because you love them, want to spend the rest of your life with them. Having children doesn't come into it.'

'It does for some women,' she said bleakly, 'and quite a few men.'

'Then they're idiots,' he retorted, and she managed a wobbly smile.

'Or human.'

He turned her hand over in his. 'How long have you been in remission?'

'Four years.'

'You do know if you get to five years then the chances of it never coming back are good?' he said, and she nodded.

'But they're not one hundred per cent certain, Hugh. I might live to be a little old lady of ninety-seven. I might die next year.' She slipped her hand out of his, even though she didn't want to, even though her hand felt cold without his wrapped round it. 'So, you see, I can't accept a permanent post anywhere. It wouldn't be fair.'

'You think Malcolm or I would withdraw our offer because of what you've told me?' he protested. 'Alex, I made you an offer of a partnership, and the offer still stands.'

'I...I appreciate that,' she said, 'but the answer's still no.'

She tried to stand up but he put his hands on her shoulders and made her sit down again.

'And what if I repeat what I said before?' he said. 'That I want you to stay. Not just for the practice, but for me?'

There was tenderness in his eyes, but not just tenderness. She could see desire there, too. A hot and devastating and completely naked desire that made her heart kick up into her throat, and her pulses begin to race, and she wanted so much to reach out and touch his face, but she mustn't, because she couldn't give him a future, she couldn't give him children, and he was a man who deserved both.

Blindly she shook her head. 'Hugh, don't, please don't.'

'Don't what?' he demanded. 'Don't say I'm attracted to

you, don't say that I want you? I can't not say it, Alex, because I do want you, you know I do.'

'Perhaps you think you want me right now,' she said, her voice trembling, 'but what you're actually feeling is pity.'

'Don't you *dare* suggest that,' he thundered. 'Yes, I feel pity for you if you mean I wish to God you'd never had to go through the treatment for Hodgkin's alone, but pity sure as hell isn't the emotion I feel when I look at you. Since that night, when you danced, all I've wanted is to hold you, to touch you, and I want…' He reached out and cradled her face in his hands. 'I want very much—if you'll let me—to make love to you.'

'Hugh…I…I…'

She couldn't say any more. Without warning, tears began to trickle down her cheeks. Tears that splashed onto his hands, and he gazed at her with dismay.

'Oh, Alex, *leannan*, don't,' he said. 'I'm sorry—so sorry. I didn't mean to upset you. I wouldn't upset you for the world.'

'It isn't you,' she said, her voice choked. 'I don't know why I'm crying. I honestly don't know why I'm crying.'

'Maybe it's something you should have done a long time ago,' he said, drawing her to him gently, but her tears didn't stop, they kept on falling, soaking into his shirt.

'I'm sorry—so sorry,' she hiccuped. 'Breaking down like this, soaking your shirt.'

'And like either of those things are an issue, right now,' he murmured, placing a kiss on the top of her head, and sliding his hands up her back to bring her closer.

I should stop this, she thought, as she clung to him, never wanting to let him go. I should simply blow my nose, and thank him for his kindness, and stop this, but it felt so good to be held, so comforting to be held, and she didn't want him to go, not yet.

'This is why you were so upset at the Nolan's, isn't it?' he said into her hair. 'Because Irene's situation reminded you so much of your own, except Frank Nolan didn't walk away from Irene. He stayed.'

She nodded into his chest, and he tightened his grip on her.

'I'm not going to walk away, Alex. I'm here for the long term, if you'll let me be.'

She wanted to believe him, she so wanted to believe him, but her doubts spoke louder.

'Alex.'

Slowly she lifted her head to meet his gaze.

'I would like very much to kiss you,' he said softly, his eyes dark, hot. 'May I kiss you?'

No, her brain whispered. *No*, every particle of common sense that she possessed warned, but her body wasn't listening to her mind or to her common sense. Her body wanted him to kiss her, even though she knew that this could only end in disaster, her body was longing for him to kiss her, and she gave a tiny, almost imperceptible nod, and he cupped her face again and then his lips met hers.

Met hers in a kiss that warm and tender, and tantalisingly brief. So brief that it was she who leant towards him, wanting more, and he kissed her again, deeper, harder, and when his tongue slipped inside her mouth, she felt the heat go everywhere.

'I have wanted to do this for so long,' he said, his lips leaving hers to trace the contours of her face, his voice ragged. 'My water sprite, my beautiful water sprite.'

Don't talk, she thought, don't give me time to think, because if I think I'll know I shouldn't be doing this, that I'm going to be hurt all over again, so don't talk, and her lips found his to silence him, and she pressed herself against him, wanting more so much more, even though it was she knew it was a mistake.

'Alex, oh, Alex,' he said huskily as he slid his hands up underneath her baggy sweatshirt to cup her breasts through the fine cotton of her bra. 'Stop me soon, or soon I'm not going to be able to stop.'

She didn't want him to stop. Her breasts ached for the touch of his hands and mouth, she could feel a hot slippery rush between her legs and, before she could think about what she was doing, she pulled her sweatshirt over her head and let it fall to the floor but when she reached for the clasp of her bra, he stayed her hands.

'Alex, are you sure about this?' he said, his eyes dark, liquid. 'Say now, if you're not sure, because…'

She didn't say anything. She couldn't because she knew if she spoke the spell would be broken, and she didn't want the spell to be broken. She simply wanted him, and she reached for him again and kissed him hard to shut out the clamouring voices in her head that told her that what she was doing could only end in heartbreak.

CHAPTER SIX

THERE was a damp patch on the wall just underneath her bedroom window-sill. It was funny how she'd never noticed it before, Alex thought, as she stared at it but then normally she just fell asleep as soon as her head hit the pillow and didn't wake until she staggered out of bed the next morning. Normally, she hadn't been lying awake since dawn, with a man's arm round her waist, wondering what the man was going to say when he woke up, and what she was going to say in reply.

Carefully, she turned in Hugh's arm, and a wistful sigh broke from her. He looked so vulnerable lying beside her, his eyelashes dark smudges on his cheeks, his lips slightly curved as though he was smiling at something, and tentatively she stretched out her hand to him only to freeze as Hugh's eyes slowly opened.

For a second he looked confused, then the corners of his mouth lifted.

'So it wasn't a dream?' he said softly.

'No, it wasn't a dream,' she managed to reply.

He reached out and touched her cheek, and it took all of her self-control not to put her hand over his simply so she could touch him back.

'I didn't want to wake up in case it was a dream,' he murmured. 'I didn't want to open my eyes to discover I was alone, in my own bed, and had simply had the most amazingly vivid, X-rated dream.'

'X-rated, huh?' she said before she could stop herself, and the smile on his lips widened.

'Maybe I've just led a very sheltered life,' he said, his fingers leaving her cheek and sliding down her naked shoulder, making her shiver, 'but that was pretty much my take on last night. Was it yours?'

'It was wonderful,' she admitted. 'You know it was.'

He searched her face for a second, then shook his head.

'But?' he prompted.

'But nothing,' she hedged, wanting to postpone the inevitable. The moment when he'd kiss her, say he'd had a great time, then walk away. 'There is no "but".'

'Yes, there is. I heard it in your voice,' Hugh said. 'What's wrong, Alex?'

'Nothing—absolutely nothing,' she protested, feeling her cheeks burn with the lie. 'Last night was fabulous, terrific, and I'd be more than willing to do it again while I'm here in Kilbreckan. If you want to, that is,' she added hurriedly. 'I mean, I understand completely that us making…' She stumbled over the words. 'Us making love involves no commitment from you, no strings, because you still love Jenny, and…'

Her voice trailed away as she saw Hugh's face slowly change from bewilderment to anger.

'No commitment,' he repeated furiously. 'No strings. You think I would have made love to you last night if I hadn't been prepared to make some sort of commitment to you?'

'Hugh—'

'Alex, last night wasn't simply about sex, at least not for me,' he exclaimed, talking over her. 'The sex might have been amazing, but that's not why I'm here, right now, beside you. Yes, I loved Jenny, I always will, but that doesn't mean there's no room in my heart for someone else.'

'For someone else, yes,' she said sadly, 'but not for me. Hugh, you don't have to pretend,' she continued as he tried to interrupt. 'I know we don't have a future. I have Hodgkin's, and last night didn't change that, so I'm content with just the now.'

'Content with just the now,' he echoed, then swore colourfully. 'Well, I sure as hell am not. You say you have Hodgkin's, and last night didn't change that. Well, I have black hair, and grey eyes, and last night didn't change that either.'

'It's not the same, you know it's not,' she said impatiently.

Hugh stared silently at her for a moment, then pushed himself up in the bed until his back was leaning against the headboard, and pulled her up beside him.

'OK, I'm clearly missing something here,' he said as he tucked the sheet neatly around her, 'so can you tell me—in words of one syllable—why you having Hodgkin's should automatically mean we can't have a future together?'

'Because…' She swallowed hard. 'Because, having gone through the pain of losing Jenny, you can't honestly want to go through that again.'

'No, I don't,' he replied, 'but neither do I want to go through the rest of my life never seeing you again, never holding you again, or making love with you again, so as you come with a diagnosis of Hodgkin's I'll have to face your cancer with you if—*if*—it comes back.'

'But—'

'Alex, do you think Frank Nolan will ever walk away from his wife?'

She bit her lip.

'She didn't have MS when they met,' she muttered. 'He didn't know what lay ahead, you do.'

'Which means I'm going into this with my eyes wide open—no deceit, no unexpected surprises.'

She couldn't prevent her lips from curving into an uneven smile. 'You know, if you hadn't become a doctor, you would have made a very good lawyer.'

'Because I'm telling you the truth?' He reached for one of her hands and laced his fingers with hers. 'Alex, there are no certainties in life. Hale, hearty, and completely healthy people are run over, fall off stepladders, and electrocuted by faulty wiring every day. In fact, it's more than likely I'll die before you do.'

'Don't say that,' she protested, feeling her heart clutch at even the thought. 'Not even as a joke.'

'I didn't mean it as a joke,' he replied. 'I'm being serious. I could walk out that door this morning, and be killed in a car crash. None of us know how long we will live, Alex, and no matter how long—or short—your life is I want to be in it with you. The big question is, do you want to be a part of my life?'

She pleated the sheet he had tucked around her for a moment, and when she spoke her voice was unsteady.

'I do want that, more than anything, but…' Her face crumpled. 'I'm *scared*, Hugh. Scared to allow myself to get close to someone again. Scared I'll hurt you by dying, scared you'll leave me because I'll get sick again, or you'll suddenly decide you want children.'

'Alex, just living is scary,' he said, drawing her into his arms so that her head was resting on his bare chest, 'and I'm scared too. Scared of losing you, scared of you maybe one day being in pain, and me not being able to help you, but I'm more scared of you walking away from me when I've only just found you.'

'Then maybe…' She swallowed hard. 'Maybe we should stop this now, before either of us get in too deep.'

'Oh, hell, *leannan*,' he said, cupping her chin and forcing her to look up at him. 'We're already in too deep, you know we are.'

'You called me that last night,' she said uncertainly. '*Leannan*. What does it mean?'

'Sweetheart in the Gaelic,' he murmured, smoothing her spiky hair down, 'and that's what you are, my *leannan*. Alex, I didn't plan for this to happen. I never expected that my waiting-room door would one day open, and you'd walk into my life.'

'You wanted me to walk right back out again,' she pointed out.

'I didn't know you then, and I didn't want to know you, but, Alex…' His lips crinkled into a warm and tender smile. 'You're a part of my life now, a part I'm not prepared to let go.'

Reluctantly, she eased herself out of his arms, and took a shuddering breath.

'You still don't know me—not really,' she said. 'You only know what you see, what I choose to let you see, and that isn't the real me.'

'You don't know the real me, either,' he observed. 'Like I'm normally crotchety as hell first thing in the morning until I've had at least two cups of coffee, that I always squeeze the toothpaste in the middle, and I snore if I lie on my back.'

'Really?' she said, unable to prevent a small snort of laughter breaking from her, and he nodded.

'Really,' he said. 'It's going to be a journey of discovery for both of us, Alex, so if you have any deep, dark secrets, now's the time to reveal them.'

The laughter faded from her face.

'Hugh…'

'Alex, you don't have to tell me anything,' he said quickly, his eyes soft and gentle. 'I was only joking. The past is over, gone. When Jenny died, I never thought I would ever feel this way again—whole and complete—but you've done this. You've achieved this miracle, simply by being you.'

'But—'

'Let go, Alex,' he said, taking both of his hands in hers. 'Let go of the past. Today is the start of a new life for both of us, a life we're going to take one day at a time, and if the cancer comes back we'll deal with that, too, one day at a time, together.'

'You make it sound so easy,' she murmured, and he smiled.

'It is, if you'll only allow yourself to believe you have a future. I didn't believe I had one. I couldn't look forward, only back, but now I'm looking forward, believing in the future again, and that's what you have to do.'

She managed a crooked smile.

'That's the hard part,' she said. 'Believing.'

'Alex, do you trust me?'

She stared up into his quicksilver eyes. She wanted to, she so wanted to, but she couldn't forget how much she had loved Jonathan and yet when she'd needed him the most he had walked out of her life.

'I want to, Hugh,' she said, 'I truly want to, but...'

'You're still scared.' He nodded. 'Then it's going to be my aim in life to have you one day say to me, "Hugh, I do trust you, no qualification."'

Her eyes began to swim, and she had to swallow hard before she could answer him.

'It might take you rather a long time to achieve that,' she said with difficulty.

'We have all the time in the world,' he said, and she didn't say the obvious.

That neither of them knew how much time they might have.

'Can I tell Malcolm and Chrissie you have Hodgkin's?' Hugh continued, and quickly she shook her head.

'No, please, I'd rather you didn't,' she said, and he caught hold of her shoulders.

'Alex, it's nothing to be ashamed of,' he protested. 'It's a part of you, and if you should ever feel very tired—'

'I don't want any special treatment,' she interrupted, and he smiled ruefully.

'You and your damned independence. Alex, people worrying about you, caring about you, doesn't weaken you. In fact, it can give you strength to help you through the bad times.'

Or devastate you if they don't help as you expect them to, she thought, but she didn't say that.

'Maybe you're right,' she said instead, 'but I still don't want you to tell them, at least not yet. I don't…I can't handle pity.'

He sighed.

'Sympathy and understanding aren't pity, Alex, but if that's what you want, I won't tell them. Can I at least tell Malcolm you've changed your mind, that you're staying on with us in the practice?'

'Hugh, can't we wait a little?' she said. 'At the moment I feel…'

She stared helplessly at him, and he smiled.

'That I'm rushing you,' he finished for her. 'I'm sorry. You're usually the impetuous one, aren't you, and now it's me being a bulldozer. I just want the whole world to know about us, but I promise I'll say nothing. Which doesn't mean, however,' he continued, his fingers beginning to gently loosen the sheet around her, 'that I'm not going to take you up on your offer that you'd be more than willing to…'

'Hugh, we can't,' she protested, as the sheet slid down to her waist, and he cupped her breasts and her nipples hardened instantly. 'We have to go to work soon, and you must want something to eat. I've cereal, fruit juice, eggs and—'

'Not hungry for breakfast,' he said, trailing a line of kisses down her neck.

'I'm hungry. I've always been a very…a very… Oh.' She

gasped, as he sucked on her breast and she felt the pull go everywhere.

'A very what?' he said huskily, as his lips began to travel slowly south.

'Eater…. Hearty….eater,' she managed, complete sentences eluding her, as she threaded her fingers through his hair and arched against him.

He raised his head, and grinned at her.

'Me, too, but I still don't want breakfast,' he said.

She didn't either, she decided, as he resumed his downward path, and she squirmed beneath him, wanting more than just his lips teasing and tantalising her. He'd said this morning that he wanted to be a part of her life. He'd said he wanted her despite her Hodgkin's, and if he hadn't mentioned the fact that she couldn't have children he'd said last night that you didn't marry somebody because you wanted children.

It'll be all right, she told herself, as he slipped between her thighs and she opened for him, wanting him hard and solid inside her. He'd told her all she had to do was believe, and she would try her best to, and this time it would be all right.

'Why, Alex, you look lovely this morning!' Chrissie exclaimed when she walked into the surgery. 'Malcolm,' she continued, seeing her husband come out of his room, 'doesn't Alex look lovely?'

'Good enough to eat.' Malcolm nodded, and Alex blushed.

'It's just an old skirt and blouse,' she said, awkwardly smoothing the folds of her blue woollen skirt down, then nervously touching the neckline of her blouse. 'I just thought I'd wear something different today as I'm not on home visits and could walk to work.'

'Well, you look gorgeous,' Chrissie declared. 'Has Hugh seen you yet?'

Alex shook her head, feeling suddenly a little self-conscious. She'd insisted on him leaving for work before her, and though Hugh had protested, pointed out that nobody would think it was odd if they arrived together, she'd managed to make him go eventually. It was after he'd gone, when she'd reached for her sweater and jeans, that she'd paused, and on impulse had extracted the skirt and blouse from her rucksack.

'You don't think people will think it peculiar, me always having worn casual clothes before, and now I'm wearing this?' she said uncertainly, and Chrissie smiled.

'They'll just see what I see,' the receptionist replied. 'A very attractive young woman.'

Alex didn't know about attractive, but by the time her morning surgery was almost over she was heartily sick to death of watching her patients do a double take every time they walked into her consulting room.

'Anyone would think I'd suddenly sprouted two heads,' she complained when she went through to Chrissie to see who was next on her list, and the receptionist laughed.

'I guess people are just accustomed to seeing you wearing one thing,' she replied, 'and any kind of change throws them. Here you go,' she continued, holding out a folder. 'Your last patient of the morning. Ellie Dickson.'

Alex's eyebrows rose. The last time she'd seen the woman she'd tried to impress upon her that regular check-ups were vital now she was in the last trimester of her pregnancy, but Ellie had made it equally plain that she considered examinations a complete waste of time so it had to be something serious to have got her here today.

'Did she give you any idea of what was wrong?' she asked, and Chrissie shook her head.

'She just said she wanted to talk to you about something.'

Ellie did, and by the time the young mother-to-be had fin-ished Alex couldn't hide her disbelief.

'Ellie, you cannot possibly be serious,' she protested. 'There is no way either I, or Dr Hugh, would sanction a home birth for you, not with your past history.'

'But you said yourself my blood pressure was fine,' Ellie exclaimed. 'And I've had none of the headaches, blurred vision or tummy pains that you will insist on interrogating me about every time you see me.'

'Yes, but—'

'I hated the hospital when I was in there, giving birth to Thomas,' Ellie continued determinedly. 'It was so big, and impersonal, and I never saw the same doctor twice, or the same nurse.'

'Whether you hated it or not, the hospital is where you're going,' Alex said firmly. 'Ellie you developed pre-eclampsia during your last pregnancy—'

'I haven't developed it this time.'

'You still could,' Alex countered. 'I'm sorry, Ellie, but this idea is a complete no-brainer. Dr Hugh would go through the roof if he knew you were even contemplating it, and I can't say I'd blame him.'

'I thought you'd understand,' Ellie protested. 'You're so much more modern than Dr Hugh and Dr Malcolm, what with your bike and everything, I thought you'd understand.'

'I do, Ellie,' Alex replied, 'but even if I thought you were a suitable candidate for a home birth—and you most cer-tainly are not—it's far too late to make the necessary arrange-ments. You don't have a birth plan worked out, or a home midwife booked—'

'So, you're saying no,' Ellie interrupted, outrage plain on her face. 'Even though this is what I want, and it's my baby, and my body, you're still saying no.'

'I'm sorry, Ellie, but, yes, I'm saying no,' Alex declared, and the girl straightened mutinously in her seat.

'I could still have a home birth,' she said. 'When I go into labour, if I don't phone for an ambulance—'

'Don't you dare even consider doing such a thing,' Alex exclaimed in horror. 'Ellie, I can appreciate your reluctance to go into hospital, but I want your solemn promise that you'll phone for an ambulance the minute you have your first contraction.'

The young woman said nothing, and Alex got to her feet, and quickly came round the side of her desk towards her.

'Ellie, please. I won't be able to sleep nights if you don't give me your promise. Think of your baby. What if either you or your baby suddenly needs expert medical help and you're at home, miles away from that help?'

Ellie bit her lip, then sighed.

'OK, all right, if it means that much to you, I promise I'll go into hospital when the time comes. You know, you're as bad as Dr Hugh,' she continued truculently. 'Fuss, fuss, fuss.'

'I'll take that as a compliment.' Alex laughed, and Ellie's lips twitched slightly.

'Actually, you *are* very like him,' the woman observed. 'Maybe all country doctors come out of a mould with *Dedicated to My Patients* stamped on them.'

'Maybe they do,' Alex said, laughing again, but when Ellie had left she sat for a moment in her consulting room, lost in thought.

Perhaps she *was* a country doctor. She'd worked in big cities, large towns and small villages in the past, and had always felt most at home in the small villages, and Kilbreckan... Everyone had been so welcoming, everyone had made her feel as though she belonged. Yes, there were drawbacks, in that anonymity was impossible, but she liked the people, the scenery and the slower pace of life.

And if Hugh Scott wasn't here? her mind demanded. Would you still like it?

'Yes, I would,' she said out loud, surprising herself. 'I actually would.'

Which meant that all she had to do was to find the courage to accept Hugh's offer of a partnership with him and Malcolm. To believe Hugh when he said she had a future, here, with him.

'Big leap of faith, Alex,' she muttered.

One day at a time, Hugh had said. Take it one day at a time.

Maybe he was right. Maybe it was possible to start anew, to look forward and not always look back, and she got to her feet with a smile and walked through to Reception, and saw Hugh deep in conversation with Chrissie.

The receptionist smiled at her round his shoulder, and she must have said something to Hugh because he turned.

'Chrissie tells me you look very…' His voice trailed off as he stared at her.

'Very what?' Alex prompted.

'Nice this morning,' he said with enough tension in his voice to make it an understatement.

'Nice, huh?' Alex said, then some mischievous impulse made her add, 'Wow, but never let it be said that a highlander doesn't know how to give a woman a fulsome compliment.'

She heard Chrissie choke down a laugh but, when she tried to hand her Ellie's folder, Hugh barred her way.

'Could I have a word, Dr Lorimer?' he said.

'A word?' she repeated, and saw a gleam appear in his grey eyes, a gleam that made her heart pick up speed. 'What about?'

'Not here, in my consulting room.'

'You still have one more patient, Hugh,' Chrissie reminded him. 'Donna Ferguson.'

'I know, but I really do need a word with Dr Lorimer,' he

declared, nudging Alex with his finger so she automatically walked ahead of him, and into his room.

'So what's this word you want to have with me?' she said, as he shut his consulting-room door.

'Show, don't tell, Lorimer,' he murmured. 'Didn't anybody ever tell you that?'

She didn't even get a second to think about what he'd said. Before she could move, before she could say anything, he had wrapped his arms around her, and, as his lips met hers, the world spun away, and she fell into him, losing track of time, of everything, except the safety of his arms, and the heat his lips were generating through her.

'W-what was that for?' she stammered, breathless and dizzy and aching for more, when he finally released her.

'Because it's been exactly two hours and fifty-three minutes since I last kissed you,' he said, his breathing as ragged as hers.

'You've been counting?' she said, and his eyes darkened.

'You bet I have,' he said, reaching for her again, and she backed away.

'Hugh, we can't. You know Chrissie never knocks unless we have a patient with us.'

He swore under his breath.

'I should have had locks fitted to these doors,' he said, and Alex couldn't help but laugh.

'That would certainly cause a few comments in the pub,' she observed. 'Maybe it might be safer if I go back to wearing my leathers if a skirt and blouse turns you on like this.'

'Everything about you turns me on,' he said, and her heart quickened as his eyes drifted over her. 'The skirt and blouse... Are they for me?'

She thought about it, then slowly shook her head. 'Actually, no, they're not. They're for me.'

'I'm glad. I mean, I'm obviously glad for myself, too, because I can't see your legs often enough,' he continued as she stared at him, puzzled, 'but I'm more pleased you decided to put those clothes on for yourself. It means you're moving on.'

'Wearing a skirt and blouse is moving on?' she exclaimed. 'Hugh, that doesn't make any sense.'

'When was the last time you wore either?'

She had to think long, and hard. 'Four—maybe a bit more—years ago,' she said, 'but I still don't see—'

'It was before your chemo, wasn't it?' he observed. 'Before then, I'm guessing you wore your leathers when you were out on your bike, but you also had a wardrobe full of pretty clothes for work. After your chemo—after Jonathan—you started hiding behind your jeans and sweatshirts, not wanting anyone to notice you're a woman, but now...'

'I'm moving on,' she murmured, then chuckled a little shakily as he nodded. 'Maybe you should have specialised in psychiatry, Hugh.'

'Nah.' He grinned. 'I just know you. Now, get out of here before I forget all about Chrissie and rip off your clothes and make love to you.'

'Rip off my clothes, huh?' she said, moistening her lips, and saw his eyes grow hot. 'Sounds good to me.'

'Alexandra Lorimer, you are playing with fire.'

'Sorry,' she said, not meaning it, and knew from the answering gleam in his eyes that he knew she didn't mean it. 'I had Ellie Dickson in this morning, and what she wanted should well and truly dampen your libido.'

'How so?' he said.

'She wanted us to sanction a home birth for her.'

'She wanted...' Hugh gazed heavenwards in disbelief. 'Of all the crackpot, completely insane... I'll have a word with her husband,' he continued grimly. 'I'll terrify the living daylights out of Geordie with a list of all the things that could happen to both Ellie and the baby if things go wrong, and that should put the kibosh on the idea.'

'I told her she should think of all the things that could go wrong, too, and she told me I was too much like you,' Alex declared, then her lips curved. 'And she didn't mean it as a compliment.'

'I bet she didn't,' Hugh said ruefully, and Alex laughed.

'I suppose—if I can be fair,' Alex observed, 'I can see why she's not overly keen to go into hospital. Maternity wards have become increasingly hi-tech over the past ten years, and a recent poll has suggested that some women are feeling dehumanised by the experience.'

'I know, but if Ellie was my wife I'd tie her to the hospital bed myself if the doctors said it was in her best interests to be there.'

He undoubtedly would, she thought, with a wry, inward chuckle.

'I'd better go,' she said. 'Donna Ferguson must be wondering what's happened to you.'

'She must, but before you go I want you to read this first,' Hugh said, retrieving a sheet of paper from his desk and holding it out to her. 'It's the results of Donna Ferguson's serum transferrin saturation test.'

Alex took the paper from him, read through it quickly, and a delighted smile lit up her face.

'Fifty-two per cent. Her iron levels are fifty-two per cent higher than they should be, so she *does* have haemochromatosis.'

He nodded. 'We have a result, and it's all down to you.'

'Nonsense,' she protested. 'All I did was make a suggestion, and my suggestion could just as easily have been wrong.'

'That's two you've won for us since you've been here,'

Hugh said. 'Lady Soutar and Donna Ferguson. Actually, three if you count Ewan Allen, and I would definitely count him.'

'Donna was a lucky guess, Lady Soutar I won over because she loves bikes, and you saved Ewan's foot,' she said firmly. 'And anyway, medicine isn't a competition, Hugh,' she added as he tried to interrupt. 'We're here to help people, not to score points off one another. It's teamwork.'

'And we make a good team, don't we?' he said. 'Malcolm, and me, and you.'

His eyes were fixed on her, and she laughed.

'Is this part of your commercial for working in Kilbreckan?' she said, and he smiled.

'Is it succeeding?' he said.

'Maybe—perhaps,' she said, and his smile widened.

'One day at a time, Alex, one day at a time,' he said, but as she turned to leave he added quickly, 'Look, why don't you stay, see Donna with me? It seems only fair as you suggested what might be wrong with her.'

'I'd like that,' she said.

Donna clearly didn't care one way or the other when she walked wearily in and sat down. In fact, she had a very obvious *And what are you going to say is wrong with me, today?* expression on her face, an expression which changed to one of complete disbelief when Hugh told her what the blood tests had revealed.

'I'm sorry, Doctor,' she declared, 'but I honestly don't see how I can have this haemochr…haemach—'

'Haemochromatosis,' Hugh finished for her. 'It *is* rather a large word, but all it really means is your body is absorbing too much iron from the food you're eating.'

'It doesn't matter whether it's a big word, or a little one,' Donna exclaimed. 'If this disease is an inherited thing, I can't possibly have it because my mother didn't, and my father hasn't.'

'Your father certainly hasn't,' Hugh agreed, 'but your mother must have but she died before she could develop it.'

'I…I'm sorry, but I don't understand,' Donna declared, and Alex leant towards her quickly.

'The reason it's taken us so long to discover what's wrong with you is that haemochromatosis often doesn't usually show up in women until they hit the menopause,' she said. 'While you were menstruating—having a period every month—you lost all the excess iron you were absorbing every month, but once you reached the menopause, you stopped bleeding, and that's when the iron started to build up in your body.'

'But I thought having a lot of iron in your body was good,' Donna said uncertainly. 'A friend of mine's anaemic, and I know how dangerous that can be, but—'

'While anaemia is certainly bad for you,' Hugh interrupted, 'having too much iron in your body is equally serious because the excess ends up being stored in your liver, heart and pancreas, and over a period of time this excess iron can seriously damage those organs if it isn't removed.'

Donna swallowed. 'You're saying I'm going to die.'

'Of course I'm not,' Hugh exclaimed. 'But it does mean we'll have to take blood from you regularly. The procedure is called a phlebotomy, and is very similar to what would happen if you were a blood donor. To begin with I'll probably have to take a pint of blood from you twice a week, but in a year or so, once your iron levels have returned to normal, I think we'll only need to perform the procedure four times a year.'

She hadn't heard him. Alex could see from the look on Donna's face that all the woman had taken in had been the words 'damaged organs'.

'Donna, haemochromatosis isn't a life-threatening condition if you follow our instructions,' she exclaimed. 'It will be inconvenient for you, having to give blood regularly, and there'll be some things you'll have to cut back on in your diet like red meat, cereals, beans and pasta because they contain iron, but if you're careful you should be able to live a virtually normal life.'

'That's easy for you to say,' Donna flared. 'You've not just been told that if you don't get on top of this disease, you're going to damage vital parts of your body, and then you'll die.'

'Donna, I know how you feel,' Alex began, and the woman shook her head vehemently, tears welling in her eyes.

'No, you don't, you can't possibly,' she exclaimed. 'I have daughters, Doctor. What if I've passed this thing on to them?'

'We can test them—'

'And that's supposed to make everything all right, is it?' Donna protested. 'I don't want them to need to be tested. I don't want to have blood taken from me twice a week forever more. I don't want to have this disease at all.'

'I know you don't,' Alex declared. 'Look, I know being told you have haemochromatosis has knocked you for six—'

'*How* do you know?' Donna interrupted, tears beginning to trickle down her cheeks. 'You've probably never had a day's illness in your life, so don't tell me you understand, because you don't.'

Alex glanced helplessly across at Hugh. He was sitting back in his seat, watching her, his face completely unreadable. She could help Donna, she knew she could, but she had always kept what was wrong with her a secret, felt it was private, her business, and her business alone.

'Donna…'

'I'm sorry, Doctor,' the woman replied, wiping her face with the back of her hand. 'I know you're trying to be kind, but the last thing I want is somebody telling me they understand when you and I both know that you can't, not ever.'

Alex straightened in her seat.

'Actually, I *can* understand,' she said. 'Not about haemo-chromatosis, but four years ago I was diagnosed with Hodgkin's lymphoma. It's a type of cancer,' she continued as Donna gazed at her blankly, 'and I had to have chemotherapy and radiotherapy. It wasn't pleasant, and I don't know whether the cancer will come back or not, but I'm still here, taking one day at a time, and that's what you'll have to do.'

'But…' Donna Ferguson gazed at her in amazement '…you look so…so normal, so healthy.'

'Because I am—touch wood,' Alex said, meeting Hugh's gaze, and he gave her a tiny way-to-go smile. 'And you will be, too, Donna, if you do what Dr Hugh says.'

'And what Dr Hugh says,' he declared, getting to his feet, 'is that there's no time like the present for your first phlebotomy.'

As Hugh had explained, it was a painless, if time-consuming procedure, and, though Donna clearly felt a little shaky and light-headed after it was over, she also looked less stressed when she left.

'I'm going to have to tell Chrissie and Malcolm now, aren't I?' Alex said ruefully when she and Hugh were alone. 'Because by tonight half of Kilbreckan is going to know I have Hodgkin's.'

'Not half,' Hugh observed. 'A quarter, I'd say, and probably a half by tomorrow morning.' He caught and held her gaze. 'Are you sorry about what you did?'

Alex said nothing for a moment, then frowned slightly.

'It was odd telling her, almost as though I was talking about someone else, but, if I helped, it was worth it.'

'Oh, it helped, all right,' he replied, 'but it took a lot of guts to do what you did, and I'm proud of you.'

'Hey, after baring my skinny legs to the world, telling Donna about my illness was a breeze,' she said, laughing a little shakily, and Hugh shook his head.

'No, it wasn't.' He looked down, and grinned. 'And your legs aren't skinny. They're svelte, slender, lithe, and I'd better stop now…'

She gazed at him severely. 'If my skinny legs turn you on, then you need therapy.'

'No, I just need you,' he said, and saw her eyes become a little hesitant, a little uncertain.

'Hugh…'

'I'm going too fast for you, aren't I?'

'Just a bit.' She nodded.

He wondered how she would react if he told her how he really felt. That when she'd told him about her Hodgkin's his heart had filled with such pain at the thought of what she'd been through, such anger at Jonathan for leaving her, and all he'd wanted to do was wrap his arms around her, to keep her safe, for always.

She'd said she was scared, but he was scared, too. Not of her illness. If it came back he'd be there, at her side, fighting it with her, taking her to every expert there was in the country, trying every possible treatment. What he was scared of was that she might still walk away. She'd given him no promise that she would stay on here, hadn't even said she wouldn't take part in the Lisbon to Dakar rally. All she had said was she would try to believe, try to trust him, whereas he…

He knew he was falling in love with her, had been gradually, unsuspectingly, falling in love with her since she'd first walked into his life.

Take it slowly, Hugh, he told himself. If you don't take it slowly, you'll lose her, but he wasn't a patient man by nature, and the thought of her leaving…

'What's wrong?'

He glanced down to see Alex staring up at him with a puzzled frown, and forced himself to smile.

'Just thinking,' he said, and she laughed.

'Dangerous occupation, thinking,' she said, and he shook his head.

'It depends on what you're thinking about,' he said, and saw a faint blush appear on her cheeks.

She'd obviously misunderstood him, imagined he was thinking about them making love, but it was better if she misunderstood him, at least for now. He'd told her she had to take life one day at a time, but he was going to have to do the same, or he knew there was a very real danger he would lose her completely.

But not immediately, he thought, when he drove her home that evening, and Alex got out of the car, then stopped dead.

'My bike,' she said, anguish plain in her voice. 'Hugh, where's my bike?'

Sgt Tulloch came quickly, but he sighed after Alex had given him all the details.

'You said you didn't lock the back wheel of your bike last night?'

'I always do—I mean I normally do,' Alex replied, 'but I was a bit preoccupied last night.'

With the Nolans, and then with me, Hugh thought, and knew Alex was thinking the same as she glanced at him.

'Can you think of anyone who's been showing a great interest in your bike recently?' the policeman continued. 'Or someone who might have a grudge against you, could have taken your bike out of spite?'

'I can't think of anyone I've antagonised,' Alex began. 'Most of the people I see are patients, and—'

'There was the biker you wouldn't give a prescription to,' Hugh interrupted. 'Though taking your bike because you wouldn't give him a prescription for tranquillisers seems a bit extreme.'

'There's a black market for tranquillisers in the city,' Sgt Tulloch observed, reopening his notebook, 'plus Dr Lorimer's bike could bring a tidy sum if the buyer was prepared to ask no questions. Where did this biker say he was camping?'

Alex gave him as much information as she could, but Sgt Tulloch didn't look optimistic when she'd finished.

'I've got to be honest, Doctor, and say the chances of you getting your bike back are small. The people who take bikes are either joy riders who generally smash them up pretty badly, or people stealing to sell on.'

'But you'll put a trace out for it?' Hugh said, and Sgt Tulloch nodded.

'I'll do it right away, and notify the other cops in the area, but…'

'I shouldn't hold my breath,' Alex finished for him, then bit her lip. 'That'll teach me to forget to lock it. Hopefully, my insurance will cover it, but it's going to make getting out to home visits pretty difficult.'

'Neil has an old Yamaha in his garage,' Hugh said after Sgt Tulloch had gone. 'It's not the fastest bike in the world but I'm sure he'd let you borrow it if I asked.'

'That would be great,' she murmured. 'Thanks.'

She was clearly upset but, as Hugh put his arm round her and gave her a hug, he had to work hard to keep his features schooled into an expression of sympathy. Selfishly—completely selfishly—all he could think was that unless her insurance company paid out—and with luck they would drag their heels as she'd left the bike unsecured—there was no way Alex was going to be able to put her life on the line by taking part in the Lisbon to Dakar rally.

Dear lord, but just the thought of her doing it had been enough to send cold shivers down his spine, he realised, as he ushered her into the house and now—hopefully—she wouldn't be able to. What he had to do now was to convince her to stay here with him and that, he suspected, was going to be a considerably harder task.

CHAPTER SEVEN

ALL you have to do is believe, Hugh had said, Alex thought as she smiled at Donna Ferguson who was on her way out of Hugh's consulting room after one of her twice-weekly phlebotomy sessions, and the woman beamed back. All you have to do is to start looking forward, and not back, he'd insisted as she noticed Rory Murray sitting in the waiting room, and the plumber threw her a cheeky grin, and she shook her head at him, but couldn't help but grin back.

It had been three weeks since she'd told Donna about her Hodgkin's, and by the end of the first week everyone in Kilbreckan and the surrounding area had known, and yet, after the initial *I would never have thought there was anything wrong with you, Doctor* nobody seemed to feel the need to mention it at all.

'People simply see it as another facet of you, along with your red hair and green eyes,' Hugh said, when she'd asked him about it. 'You can bet your boots everyone tore off to look it up in their home medical books—particularly Sybil Gordon—but now they know what Hodgkin's is, it's no big deal for them. You're just you, Alex.'

He'd been right, she realised, as she put the file of the last patient she'd seen in Chrissie's in-tray. Even the receptionist and her husband had treated her no differently. Malcolm had given her a hug, and Chrissie had said if there was ever anything she could do to let her know, but they hadn't crowded her, overwhelmed her with sympathy, or made her feel they were earmarking wreaths and buying black clothes. To them she was clearly just the same person as she'd been before, and it felt wonderful.

'And how is my favourite locum this morning?' a familiar deep voice murmured, and she turned with a smile.

'Just fine, thank you,' she replied. 'And how is my esteemed boss?'

'Feeling distinctly deprived,' Hugh said with a mock mournful look.

She threw him a warning glance. Chrissie might be on the phone in her office, but the surgery walls weren't thick, and Rory wasn't the only patient in the waiting room. Mrs MacDonald and her three-and-a-half-year-old twins were there, too.

'I don't know how you can possibly be feeling deprived,' she said, feeling her cheeks heat. 'Not after last night.'

'Ah, but as I told you,' Hugh said, his grey eyes dancing, 'I'm a hearty eater, and it must be at least three hours since I last kissed you.'

'And it will be at least another six hours before you can kiss me again,' she said, trying to look serious and failing completely.

'Bored with me already, are you?' He grinned.

No, not bored, she thought. In fact, sometimes it overwhelmed her when she realised how quickly he'd become a part of her life, how important that part was, and how easily Kilbreckan had come to feel like home. If it should all go wrong, if it should all suddenly shatter around her…

'Of course I'm not bored,' she said, suddenly realising that he was waiting for her to answer and that the laughter in his face had been replaced by a frown.

'You have that look on your face.'

'I don't have a bored look on my face,' she protested, and he sighed.

'Not a bored look, but that look which tells me you're thinking about the past, and I don't like that look.'

'Hugh, I wasn't—'

'Hugh—Alex.' Chrissie beamed as she came through from her office, clutching a piece of paper. 'There's a letter in from the hospital about Lady Soutar's endoscopy. Do you want to read the results before you see your next patients?'

'Do we ever,' Alex exclaimed, taking the sheet of paper the receptionist was holding out to them. Quickly she read the report, then handed it to Hugh. 'A gastric ulcer. Well, no big surprise there. Chrissie, could you phone—?'

'Already done it,' the receptionist replied. 'Lady Soutar wasn't in so I asked her housekeeper to pass on the message that her results were here, and we'd appreciate it if she could come down to the surgery to discuss them.'

'I think that's called the triumph of hope over experience,' Hugh said wryly. 'She'll demand a home visit as usual, and when she does could you try to fit it in on a day when one of us will be near Glen Dhu? Criss-crossing the country to pay her a home visit is not time effective.'

'I'll do my best,' Chrissie replied. She held out a file to him. 'Rory Murray.'

'OK,' Hugh replied, but as he turned to go he cocked an eyebrow at Alex. 'No more of those looks, and that's an order.'

'Looks?' Chrissie repeated after he'd gone. 'What looks is Hugh talking about?'

'No idea,' Alex said evasively. 'Who do I have next?' she added, but Chrissie ignored the question.

'Hugh certainly seems to be full of bounce these days, doesn't he?' she said instead, her voice casual, but her eyes sparkling with clear interest.

'Having three doctors makes a big difference,' Alex replied. 'It means everyone's less stressed and tired.'

'Uh-huh,' Chrissie said, and Alex knew the receptionist was not one bit deceived.

So much for keeping her relationship with Hugh a secret, she thought with a deep sigh. They'd been sleeping together for just three weeks, and already Chrissie had clearly guessed, but she wasn't about to confirm the receptionist's suspicions. She might have been willing to go public about her Hodgkin's, but her relationship with Hugh was not for public consumption. At least not yet.

'So, who do I have next?' she asked determinedly.

'It's the MacDonald twins for their booster MMR jabs. Mrs MacDonald—'

The receptionist bit off the rest of what she'd been about to say as the waiting-room door suddenly opened, then let out a gasp of dismay as a distinctly harassed-looking Mrs Allen appeared with Jamie by her side, blood dripping down his forehead.

'Holy mackerel, Jamie!' Alex exclaimed. 'How on earth did you do that?'

'You might well ask, Doctor,' Mrs Allen said with resignation as Alex swiftly steered Jamie through to her consulting room. 'You'd think a fractured elbow would keep him out of harm's way, but he was playing some game with his brother, Martin, caught his forehead on the sitting-room door latch, and this is the result.'

Quickly Alex reached for a bottle of antiseptic.

'This is going to sting quite a bit, Jamie,' she warned, 'but I need to see how deep the wound is.'

It was deep. In fact, the only thing to be thankful for was though the gash ran from Jamie's hairline to his eyebrow, he would have lost an eye if it had been any lower.

'It needs stitches, Mrs Allen,' Alex declared. 'Steri strips aren't going to be nearly strong enough to keep the wound together. I'll phone A and E, tell them you're on your way—'

'Can't you just stitch it for him, Doctor?' Mrs Allen interrupted. 'When Neil cut his arm a couple of years back, Dr Hugh stitched it for him, and to be honest I'm not really up for yet another visit to the hospital.'

Alex stared indecisively at the little boy. If the wound had been on his arm, or his leg, she wouldn't have thought twice, but the gash was smack bang in the middle of his forehead, and if she made the stitches just that little bit too tight he would be left with a horribly disfiguring scar.

'I'll be back in a minute, Mrs Allen,' she said. 'I just want a word with Dr Scott, so could you keep that pad against Jamie's forehead for me?'

Jamie's mother nodded, and Alex sped swiftly down to Hugh's room, praying he hadn't called Rory Murray through yet, but he had. She had to wait a good ten minutes while Rory complained that the anti-inflammatory drugs he'd been prescribed weren't working nearly as well as the paracetamol, and the physiotherapist Hugh had arranged for him to see must be related to Attila the Hun because the exercises he was expecting him to do were downright impossible.

'Not exactly the world's best patient, is he?' Alex observed when Rory had finally gone.

'He wants an instant cure, but there is no cure for osteoarthritis,' Hugh replied. 'All we can do is manage the condition.' He leant back in his seat with a smile. 'And you clearly have a problem judging by the way you shot into my room, or did you feel my irresistible charm calling to you?'

'Your charm is indisputable.' She smiled. 'But I'm afraid, on this occasion, I have a problem.'

Quickly, she told him what had happened, and he winced. 'Sounds nasty,' he said.

'It is, and I know I shouldn't ask this,' Alex said, 'but could you stitch Jamie's forehead for me? He's only six, Hugh,' she added as Hugh's eyebrows rose, 'and the last thing I want is him to be left with a really visible scar for the rest of his life.'

'Not a problem,' he declared, getting to his feet, and Alex followed him back to her consulting room with relief.

'Are you going to use toothed or non-toothed forceps?' she asked after Hugh had deadened the area he was going to stitch, and Jamie had been bribed by his mother with the promise of unlimited time on his games console if he kept still.

'I prefer the toothed variety when stitching a wound like this,' Hugh replied, 'but the most important thing to remember when stitching through skin on the forehead is to keep your wrist as flexible as possible when you insert the needle, and to use interrupted sutures for the best cosmetic effect.'

Alex didn't know about keeping her wrist flexed but, as she watched Hugh deftly insert the sutures into Jamie's forehead, she did know an expert when she saw one.

'You should have been a surgeon,' she said with admiration when he had finished.

'I did think about it,' he observed. 'Still do on days when I get patients like…when I get some patients,' he amended with a wink, 'but I prefer the continuity of patient care that being a GP brings.'

'It was Kilbreckan's lucky day when Dr Scott and Dr MacIntyre decided to set up in practice here,' Mrs Allen observed. 'I don't know what we'd do without them.'

'Flattery will get you nowhere, Grace,' Hugh said, his grey eyes twinkling, and the woman shook her head.

'I always give credit where credit is due, Dr Hugh,' she said, then sighed as she gazed at her son. 'I suppose it could have been worse, but he's certainly not going to be the bonnie laddie he was.'

'I have every hope he'll grow up to rival his big brother, Neil, in the good looks stakes,' Hugh said encouragingly as Alex helped the young boy down from her examination table. 'I know it looks a bit rough now but that's just because of the swelling and the sutures. With luck, Jamie will eventually only be left with a very faint line on his forehead.'

'If you say so, Doctor,' Mrs Allen said dubiously. 'When will he have to come back to have the stitches removed?'

'Bring him back in a week so we can take a look at them,' Hugh replied. 'They might be ready to remove, they might not. It's very much a look and see affair with stitches, but if the wound should begin to weep, or look very red and inflamed, I want him back here immediately, OK?'

'Will do, Doctor.' Mrs Allen nodded. 'And thank you, too, Dr Alex.'

'I didn't do anything,' Alex protested, and Grace Allen smiled, then shot a sidelong glance at Hugh.

'I think you'd be surprised at what you've done, lass.'

Alex could feel her cheeks prickling under Mrs Allen's steady gaze, and after Jamie and his mother had left she groaned.

'You know, our relationship has to be the worst-kept secret in Kilbreckan,' she exclaimed. 'I've already had Chrissie doing her wink wink, nudge nudge routine, and now Mrs Allen obviously suspects something. Maybe we should just put stickers on our chests saying, *Yes, we've done it,* and put an end to all the speculation.'

Hugh paused in the middle of binning the instruments he had used to stitch Jamie's forehead.

'Does the speculation bother you?' he said.

'Not bother, exactly, it's just…' Alex sighed. 'I'd really like to have some private life.'

'It's pretty well impossible to have a private life if you live in the country,' he murmured, 'but, conversely, it's also almost impossible to be lonely here. And speaking of country living…' he continued, his expression becoming carefully neutral. 'You only have another two weeks with us and then your contract will be over. If you're not going to Cumbria, you'll have to tell the agency.'

'I know.'

'Meaning?'

'Meaning, don't crowd me, Hugh, OK?' she said lightly, but it didn't mean that, and she knew it didn't.

It meant I don't know what to do, she thought as she collected the soiled swabs they'd used on Jamie. The last three weeks with Hugh had been wonderful so it should have been easy for her to say, yes, I want to stay on here, and yet still she was hesitating.

You've not even been hesitating, her mind pointed out. Hesitating suggests you've been actively thinking about it, when what you've actually been doing is pushing it to the back of your mind, simply enjoying the now.

'Alex, sometimes you just have to jump into the water,' Hugh declared softly. 'And you won't sink. I promise I'll always be there to catch you.'

She stared up at him, at the face she now knew almost as well as her own, and all of her instincts urged her to simply say, yes, she would phone the agency, tell them she was no longer available for locum work, but Jonathan's rejection had cut deep, and the wound was still there no matter how hard she tried to erase it.

'I'd better get on,' she said. 'The MacDonald twins have come in for their booster MMR jab, and you know what they're like. If they're kept waiting too long they'll start demolishing the waiting room.'

Hugh nodded as he followed her out of her consulting room, but he didn't look happy when he disappeared back into his consulting room, and she didn't blame him. He was giving everything to their relationship while she...

'Thank goodness you're here,' Chrissie said, looking distinctly harassed when Alex joined her, and Hugh disappeared into his own consulting room. 'The MacDonald twins have already emptied the toy box, knocked over every potted plant, and managed to pull down one of the curtains. Give them another five minutes and I wouldn't be surprised if they start unscrewing the waiting-room door.'

'Regular bundles of fun,' Alex said dryly, and Chrissie shook her head.

'In sore need of some severe discipline, if you want my opinion. My kids would never have been allowed to...'

Chrissie came to a halt as the waiting-room door swung open, and Alex would have been hard pressed to say later whether it was she or Chrissie who was most stunned to see who was standing on the threshold.

'Alex, my dear.' Lady Soutar beamed, advancing towards her. 'I was on my way to Kilbreckan to see the vet about one of my dogs when my housekeeper phoned me on my mobile to say you had the results of my tests and wanted to discuss them with me.'

'I— Yes—we do,' Alex stammered, still stunned by the fact that Lady Soutar had actually come in to see her.

'I know what I've got, of course,' Lady Soutar declared dismissively. 'Idiot man at the hospital maintained at first that he couldn't tell me—correct medical procedures, or some such rot—but, as I told him, it's my body so surely I have as much right—if not more—to know what's wrong with it as he does.'

'Right,' Alex replied, desperately avoiding Chrissie's eyes because she knew if she met them she would be sunk.

'What I want to know now is how we treat this blasted thing,' Lady Soutar continued, 'so, do you have a private room where we can discuss this?'

'I do, but I'm afraid you'll have to wait a few minutes,' Alex replied, seeing Chrissie wince as a high-pitched wail came from the waiting room. 'I have to give the MacDonald twins their MMR injections, but after that I'm free.'

'Splendid,' Lady Soutar said, then glanced at Chrissie. 'I'd like a white coffee, with no sugar, and two chocolate biscuits.'

'I don't…. We don't normally…' Chrissie looked in mute appeal at Alex, but Alex was too busy trying not to laugh to help her. 'A white coffee, with no sugar, you said, Lady Soutar?'

'And two chocolate biscuits.' Lady Soutar nodded, and strode into the waiting room, leaving Chrissie staring, open-mouthed, after her.

'I suppose we should be grateful she's come in and saved somebody a trip to Glen Dhu,' the receptionist said, shaking her head, 'but she really is the absolute, giddy limit.'

'With bells on,' Alex said, her eyes dancing. 'How many patients has Hugh left to see?'

'Rory Murray was his last,' Chrissie replied. 'I imagine he's probably catching up on his paperwork now. Do you want me to tell him Lady Soutar's here?'

'Do I ever,' Alex said. 'And could you tell him he's more than welcome to sit in with me when I see Lady Soutar to discuss her treatment if he wants.'

'If he wants?' Chrissie chuckled. 'Alex, I think he'd knock down your door if you tried to keep him out of this consultation.'

'He probably would.' Alex laughed. 'Tell Hugh I'll need about ten minutes with the MacDonald twins, and then I should be ready for Bunty. Oh, and don't forget,' she continued, her eyes sparkling. 'It's a white coffee—'

'With no sugar, and two chocolate biscuits,' Chrissie said, then burst out laughing.

'The gastrointestinal endoscopy was slightly uncomfortable,' Lady Soutar declared as she sat in Alex's consulting room, 'but, as I said to the consultant, once you've had a breech birth, you can pretty well stand anything.'

'I gather from Dr Lorimer that Mr Denara gave you the results of the test?' Hugh observed, his lips twitching slightly.

'Didn't want to at first—stupid man—but I soon persuaded him,' Lady Soutar exclaimed. 'Told him, my body, my results, and that's when he told me I had a gastric ulcer. Reckoned I must have had it for at least ten years, and couldn't understand why you lot hadn't picked it up, but had kept prescribing antacids.'

Hugh caught Alex's eye and she smothered a smile.

'Did Mr Denara explain what a gastric ulcer is, Bunty?' she said, and Lady Soutar rolled her eyes.

'Showed me a lot of incomprehensible diagrams, and said it was a hole in the lining of the stomach caused by acidic digestive juices but, as I said to him, I don't give two hoots about what caused it. I just want to know how to get rid of it.'

'And what did Mr Denara say?' Alex asked a little unsteadily.

'Silly chap said I had to discuss what happened next with my own GP.' Lady Soutar shook her head. 'Seems to me he was very good at making a diagnosis, but not exactly the brightest light bulb in the shop when it came to suggesting a cure. I suppose I'll have to have an operation?'

Alex glanced across at Hugh.

'In the past you most certainly would have done,' he said, 'but thanks to the work of two Australian doctors—a Dr Warren and a Dr Marshall—we now know that many ulcers are caused by a bacterium in the stomach called *Helicobacter pylori*. Actually, Dr Marshall proved that *H. pylori* caused gastric inflammation by deliberately infecting himself with the bacterium.'

'Sounds like my sort of man,' Lady Soutar said. 'Must have been a Brit before he moved down under.'

'I don't think he—'

'So how do we get rid of this ulcer?' Lady Soutar interrupted, cutting right across Hugh, and Alex had to bite down hard on her lip to quell the laughter she could feel welling in her throat. 'I presume I'll have to take some pretty potent pills to kill off the bacteria?'

'What you'll need is a course of antibiotics,' Hugh replied, 'and some acid-reducing tablets.'

Lady Soutar looked sceptical. 'And this will cure the damned indigestion that's been plaguing me?'

'It will if you complete the course,' Hugh said. 'The most important thing is not to stop taking the pills even when you feel better. Not completing the course is one of the biggest causes of antibiotics failing to work.'

'I'll tell my maid to remind me,' Lady Soutar declared, and got to her feet. 'Alex, my dear, you must pop in to Glen Dhu one afternoon soon for a chat and a coffee. Dr Scott…' Her gaze swept over him. 'You need a haircut.'

She'd swept out of the door before either Alex or Hugh could reply, and as their eyes met they both burst out laughing.

'What a woman,' Hugh said, shaking his head. 'God, but I wish I could have been there when Mr Denara performed her endoscopy. Do you reckon the poor man's in therapy now?'

'If he isn't, he definitely will be if we ever have to send Bunty back to him.' Alex laughed. 'But at least she's finally accepted that she *does* have a gastric ulcer, so hopefully that will mean no more midnight calls for you and Malcolm.'

'You mean, no more midnight calls for *us*,' Hugh declared, his eyes fixed on her, and Alex's laughter became a little shaky.

'You don't give up, do you?' she said, and he shook his head.

'Nope, and I definitely won't ever give up on you. I don't give up on the people I love.'

'Hugh…'

'I know what you're going to say,' he continued as she stared at him in amazement. 'That it's too soon for me to say I love you. That I've known you for less than three months, but I think I began falling in love with you when you clambered into Ewan Allen's van, and elbowed me in the ribs. I know I wanted you desperately after I saw you dance.'

'That—what you felt—it's just sexual attraction, Hugh,' she said awkwardly, and he smiled, a warm, tender smile, that kicked her heart up into her throat.

'Perhaps, but, Alex, do you want to know when I realised I was completely dead in the water as far as you're concerned?' he said. 'It was when you told Donna Ferguson what was wrong with you. It was then that I knew that I'd fallen in love with you, and that it wasn't going to change, not ever.'

She stared at him blindly, her throat so tight it was an actual physical pain.

'I…I don't know what to say,' she said.

'"I love you, too, Hugh," would do it,' he said.

She thought of what her life would be like if she never saw him again, and her heart shrivelled. She thought of how she would feel if anything happened to him, and such a surge of loneliness coursed through her that she almost cried out. She did love him. She was never going to love anyone as much as she loved him, and he would never let her down as Jonathan had done, she knew he wouldn't. He would always be there for her, and she opened her mouth to tell him so, and his phone rang.

Apologetically, he reached to answer it, but, as he listened to whoever was on the end of the line, Alex knew immediately that something was wrong. A deep frown had appeared on his forehead, and he was already stretching for his medical bag.

'That was Geordie Dickson,' Hugh said as soon as he'd put the phone down. 'Ellie's waters have broken, and the contractions are coming every thirty minutes.'

'She's also two to three weeks early, Hugh,' Alex said, already on her feet, and he nodded.

'It could have been worse,' he said. 'She could have been three months early. Geordie's called for an ambulance but, by the sound of it, I don't think it's going to arrive at their house in time.'

Alex knew it definitely wasn't going to arrive on time when she and Hugh arrived at Ellie's house, and Geordie rushed out to tell them that the contractions were now just ten minutes apart.

'Do you think she's been deliberately waiting, doing what she threatened to do, so she doesn't have to go to hospital?' Alex muttered as she followed Hugh into the cottage.

'Geordie says no, and I believe him,' Hugh replied in the same undertone. 'He said this baby just doesn't seem to want to wait.'

It didn't. Within five minutes of their arrival, Ellie's cervix had dilated to ten centimetres and the contractions were coming every three minutes.

'This wasn't planned,' Ellie gasped as Hugh and Alex crouched down beside her. 'I know I said I wanted a home birth, but this really, *really* wasn't planned.'

'Can't you give her gas, or air, or something?' Geordie Dickson demanded, wiping his forehead with a shaking hand, and Hugh shook his head.

'We don't have any, and even if we did, it wouldn't help because I can already see the baby's head.'

So could Alex as Hugh reached quickly forward to support it, and she caught hold of Ellie's hand and smiled encouragingly at her.

'OK, Ellie, you know the drill,' she said. 'Huff, puff, and push.'

'Easier…said…than…done,' the woman said breathlessly.

'You're doing fine, Ellie, just fine,' Alex observed, seeing Hugh giving her the thumbs-up. 'Now push again—just one more time.'

'The shoulders are out,' Hugh declared. 'Just the bottom to follow, and we're there.'

'Is it a girl or a boy?' Geordie Dickson asked, hopping from one foot to the other, his face almost as red as his wife's. 'We were hoping for a daughter, a little sister for Thomas, but right now I don't care what it is as long as it's all right.'

'It's too soon to tell,' Hugh said. 'But Ellie's certainly going for a record delivery time.'

Ellie laughed, gasped, then groaned.

'The baby's almost here, Ellie!' Alex exclaimed. 'Just one more push—a really big one.'

'Didn't you already say, "Just one more push"?' Ellie protested, her face scarlet.

Alex chuckled.

'I did. I was hoping you hadn't heard me. OK, relax… relax…now push….push… Oh, wonderful!' she declared as, with a tiny wail of protest, the baby suddenly slipped out into Hugh's waiting hands.

Quickly he clamped the umbilical cord, and cut it, and Ellie tried to lever herself upright.

'Is it all right?' she said as Hugh began massaging her stomach to help the afterbirth come away. 'Is my baby all right?'

'You have a lovely baby girl, Ellie,' Alex said, laying the baby gently beside her. 'A beautiful little sister for Thomas.'

'Isn't she gorgeous, Dr Hugh?' Geordie Dickson declared with clear delight. 'Absolutely, and completely gorgeous.'

'She is, indeed,' Hugh replied, as the baby grasped hold of his finger and held onto it tightly. 'Look at her, Alex. Look at her little fingernails, and toenails, and she's got two dimples in her cheeks.'

'You'd think you'd never seen a baby before,' Alex protested with a half-laugh, and he shook his head.

'Not a newborn. Not since I was at med school. GPs don't normally assist at home births any more, so it's a long time since I've seen a baby as small as this one.'

'Do you want to hold her, Doc?' Geordie Dickson said. 'Go on—hold her,' he insisted as Hugh gazed uncertainly at him. 'You helped her to arrive so it's only fair you should get to give her a cuddle.'

And Hugh laughed, and took the baby, and, as Alex stared at him and saw his face soften as he gazed down at the little girl, she felt something tear inside her.

She would never be able to give him this, not ever. If she stayed with him he would never be able to hold a child of his own in his arms. Never be able to bore people rigid with photographs of his son or daughter, or watch their eyes glaze over as he recounted tales of what his children had said or done. She couldn't give him the opportunity to be a delighted dad on school sports days when he wouldn't care whether his son came first or last. She couldn't give him a daughter he'd video so proudly when she was chosen to be the fifth spear holder in the back row of the Christmas nativity play.

He'd said it didn't matter, that only she mattered, but to deny him the opportunity to become a father...It would be wrong, so wrong, because he was a man who should be a father. A man who would make a terrific father, but all the IVF treatment in the world couldn't make her fertile again. Nothing could.

'I think she just smiled at me,' Hugh said with clear delight. 'Look, Alex, that's a smile, isn't it?'

'I…I think the experts would say it was just wind,' she said with difficulty.

'No, that's not wind, that's a smile,' he insisted. 'That's a lovely smile.'

'Do you want to hold her, Dr Alex?' Geordie Dickson said, turning to her, and she shook her head quickly.

I can't, I can't, she thought. Not when Hugh has just held her, not when I've seen the wonder in his eyes, the gentleness, the tenderness.

'I…I think, as she's slightly premature, maybe the fewer people who hold her the better,' she managed to say.

'Good point.' Hugh nodded as he handed the little girl back to Ellie. 'And that—if I'm not very much mistaken,' he added, as the sound of a wailing siren split the air, 'is the ambulance. A little late in the day, perhaps, but still in time to take mum and baby to the hospital.'

Ellie didn't want to go, but both Hugh and Alex insisted.

'Ellie, your daughter's three weeks premature,' Alex pointed out. 'She looks to be a good weight, and she's breathing well, but midwifery is neither my nor Dr Scott's speciality, so humour us, please?'

'OK—all right—if you think it's best for Alexandra, then we'll go,' Ellie said with a very definite sigh, and Alex gazed at her blindly.

'You…you're going to call her Alexandra?' she said, and Ellie beamed.

'Geordie and I decided about a month ago that if this little one was a girl, we'd like to name her after you.'

'I think that's a lovely gesture, don't you?' Hugh said with a smile, and Alex dug her fingernails deep into her palms to stop herself from crying out loud, and felt her heart tear just that little bit more.

No more, she thought. *Please, no more.*

'I'm hugely honoured,' she forced herself to say, 'but surely there are other, lovelier, names that you could give her?'

But the couple were adamant, and within minutes, Geordie, Ellie and baby Alexandra had been whisked into the ambulance and were gone.

'Are you OK?' Hugh asked, shooting her a puzzled glance as he drove back to the surgery.

'Fine,' she replied. 'The birth was just a bit unexpected, that's all.'

'You can say that again.' He grinned. 'But hopefully little Alexandra will be none the worse for arriving too early. And speaking of arriving too early,' he continued, 'we've yet to finish the conversation we were having before she decided to put in an appearance.'

She knew what he meant, but she didn't want to continue their conversation. No matter how she felt about him, she knew now that she couldn't stay. He would say she was being foolish, that it didn't matter to him that she could never give him children, but it mattered to her, and what if—despite all his protestations—it one day mattered to him? It was better for both their sakes if she walked away now, and she had to tell him so, and quickly.

'You've got that look on your face again,' he observed, when he drew his car to a halt outside the surgery. 'The look I don't like.'

'Hugh, we have to talk.'

'Sounds ominous,' he declared. He searched her face for a second, but clearly found no clue there, because he nodded. 'OK, come into my consulting room.'

She followed him reluctantly, knowing that she didn't want to do what she was about to do, but knowing, too, that she must.

'Hugh, I've come to a decision,' she said the moment he had closed his consulting-room door behind them. 'I'm not staying on here in Kilbreckan. What we've shared has been great, but I…' *Make it convincing, Alex, make it convincing.* 'I have these plans, you see, things I want to do, and I have to keep focused. If I allow myself to be distracted—'

'You're saying I've just been a distraction?' he interrupted, hurt plain in his face, and she stared at him aghast.

'No—no—that came out all wrong,' she exclaimed. 'What I'm trying to say is, I can't stay, and if you think about this rationally you'll see that you don't really want me to. I…' *Come up with a good reason, Alex, a really good reason.* 'I'm too much of a gadfly, always on the go, always wanting to see things, do things. You'd get irritated with me. What you see now as…as appealing, you'd find annoying in time.'

'I would never find you annoying,' he insisted. 'Alex, have I come on too strong, too fast, telling you that I love you? If it's that, I can back off, give you some space, but please… please, don't go. I don't want you to go.'

Oh, don't say that, she thought, feeling her heart clench, as his grey eyes met hers, and she could see the pain and bewilderment in them, but she mustn't weaken, she mustn't, for his sake.

'I just…Hugh, I don't want to be tied down. I want to go where I want, when I want.'

'On your own.'

'Sorry?' she said in confusion.

'Wouldn't the hang-gliding, and white water rafting, and biking, and all the rest of it be a lot more fun if you could share it with someone?' he said, and, before she could prevent him, he'd reached out and grasped her hands in his. 'I'll come with you.'

'What?' she said faintly.

'I'll throw up everything here, and come with you, and we can white water raft, or skydive, or hurl ourselves out of aeroplanes together.'

'Hugh, please—'

'Alex, I know Kilbreckan must seem quiet and dull after all the exciting places you've been to, and I…' He bit his lip. 'I probably seem a bit dull, too, but when Jenny died I never thought I'd find anyone I could love as much as I loved her, and you—'

'Don't,' she begged. 'Hugh—please—don't say any more. You're a lovely man—a very special man—but I just can't stay.'

'This is all because of Ellie Dickson's baby, isn't it?'

His eyes were suddenly dark, angry, and she shook her head.

'No.' She lied. 'It isn't.'

'When you saw Ellie's baby it reminded you that you can't have children,' he exclaimed. 'And you think if we stay together you'll be depriving me of the opportunity to become a father.'

'No—no—'

'Alex, I can keep repeating until I have no voice left to speak that it doesn't matter to me if I never have children,' he declared, his grip on her hands tightening, 'but I can't make you believe it, only you can do that, and until you do you're a coward.'

'I'm a *what*?' she gasped.

'You heard me,' he said. 'All these challenges you set for yourself—they're not real challenges because if the going gets tough, and you don't want to do them any more, you can just walk away from them.'

'I have *never* given up on a challenge that I've set myself.' She flared, driven beyond endurance. 'Whatever I start, I finish.'

'Perhaps you do,' he said, 'but, the thing is, Alex, you don't *have* to do any of them, but there are thousands of people out there in the real world who have to face real challenges every day of their lives whether they want to or not.'

'I know that, but—'

'There are people who have no jobs, no money, and no hope of ever getting either. People with disabled children, and people with loved ones who are dying. These are *real* challenges, Alex, not the made-up ones you do. What you're doing is running away from life.'

'How *dare* you?' she exclaimed, her colour high. 'I've had to face Hodgkin's on my own. My mother fell apart, and the man I loved…the man I thought wanted to marry me…he *walked*, Hugh. He walked out on me.'

'And you'll never forgive him for that, will you?'

She wanted to say he was wrong, that she understood why Jonathan had behaved as he had, but suddenly all the old hurt, and pain, and heartache that she had been keeping a lid on for years boiled over.

'No, I'll never forgive him,' she said, her voice trembling. 'I *loved* him, Hugh, and when I needed him most, when I desperately needed him to just hold me, to be there for me, he wasn't, and I will never ever forgive him for that.'

'And you think every other man you meet is going to do the same,' he said. 'You think every other man is either going to freak out if your cancer comes back, or suddenly decide he wants children.'

'I can't risk it—don't you see that?' she cried. 'I just can't take the risk.'

'Oh, *leannan*,' he said softly, his voice unbelievably tender, 'can't you see that, at the moment, you're like a seed blowing in the wind, going wherever that wind takes you, never settling anywhere, never leaving your mark anywhere?'

'What's wrong with that?' she said. 'It means I can go wherever I want, do whatever I want, be free.'

'Yes, but for a seed to grow, for it to become what it was born to be,' he protested, 'it has to put down roots or eventually it will simply wither and die.'

He was right, she knew he was, but she couldn't admit it, even though her heart was breaking.

'Hugh—'

'Alex, there are no certainties in life,' he exclaimed. 'But I, at least, am prepared to take the risk, to gamble again on love. I never thought I'd ever meet another woman to whom I could say, "Take my heart, it's yours," but you've done that, simply by being you, whereas you…' He shook his head. 'You'd rather run away to your made-up challenges than give your heart to anyone, and that isn't living, and until you can see that, accept that, you'll never truly be alive and free.'

And before she could answer he walked out of his consulting room, letting the door clatter shut in her face.

CHAPTER EIGHT

DÉJÀ VU, Hugh thought wearily, as he stared across his desk at Sybil Gordon's plump and worried face. Now he understood exactly what people meant when they said they were experiencing déjà vu.

'You've been reading your medical book again, haven't you?' he said. 'The one I told you to burn.'

A faint wash of colour appeared on Mrs Gordon's round face.

'I might have dipped into it, simply to check—'

'And what did I tell you I would do if you didn't get rid of that medical book?' Hugh interrupted, fixing Mrs Gordon with a steely gaze.

'That you'd come round to my house and burn it yourself,' Sybil Gordon said in a very small voice, and Hugh nodded.

'I want that book on your fire, or in your dustbin, by tonight. It's a danger, and a menace, and is causing you nothing but grief.'

Not to mention being quite likely to push me over the edge, he thought.

'So, you don't think I might have Lassa fever?' Sybil Gordon queried and Hugh gritted his teeth until they hurt.

'Not unless you've made a trip to West Africa that I know nothing about. You have a cold, Mrs Gordon. An ordinary, common-or-garden winter cold as does half the population of Kilbreckan at the moment.'

'Well, if you're sure that's all it is, doctor,' Sybil Gordon said, looking anything but convinced. Slowly she walked to his consulting-room door then paused. 'So, Dr Lorimer is definitely leaving us at the weekend?'

'Yes, she's definitely leaving,' Hugh replied tightly.

'I'll miss her classes,' Mrs Gordon murmured.

Which undoubtedly explained why Sybil was reading her medical book again, Hugh thought, but he didn't say that.

'The classes aren't stopping just because Dr Lorimer's leaving,' he said instead. 'Dr MacIntyre and I will be taking it in turn to weigh everyone who comes along, and Dr Lorimer has arranged for a professional belly dancer to continue to teach the dance element.'

'But it won't be the same, will it?' Mrs Gordon observed.

It wouldn't, Hugh thought, after Sybil Gordon had gone, but he'd made his feelings plain to Alex, and she'd made her feelings equally clear back. So clear, in fact, that for the past week they'd barely exchanged more than a handful of words, and all of them had been about their patients.

Hugh sighed as he gazed out of his consulting-room window at the scudding grey clouds, and bare branches swaying in the stiff, cold wind. The first snows of winter would be arriving soon, and he hated the winter. It was when Jenny had died. When he'd begun existing rather than living until a red-haired water sprite had ridden into his life. A red-haired water sprite who was lippy, and opinionated, but who had healed his broken heart, and now she was leaving on Sunday and there seemed to be nothing he could say that would make her change her mind.

'So, it's back to the way it was before, Hugh,' he said to the grey clouds. 'With an empty heart, an empty bed, and only Mrs Gordon's catalogue of ridiculous ailments to enliven your days.'

No, his heart protested. He didn't want to go back to that. Not when he'd tasted what life could be like, should be like. There had to be some way he could change Alex's mind. Some way he could reach past her defences, get her to see he'd meant every word he'd said, but *what*?

Show, not tell, Hugh, a small voice whispered at the back of his mind, and, as he stared unseeing at the clouds, a slow smile began to spread across his lips. A smile that deepened and widened as an idea took shape. An idea that was crazy, and totally insane, but…

Quickly, he got to his feet, and opened his consulting-room door.

'Chrissie, have Alex and Malcolm got any more patients?' he asked as the receptionist looked up from her desk.

'Malcolm's finished for the morning, but Alex still has Lady Soutar with her,' Chrissie replied.

'Good.' He nodded. 'Could you tell them that the post-surgery meeting will be in my room in fifteen minutes, but until then I don't want to be disturbed. I have phone calls to make.'

And some very serious phone calls at that, he thought with a smile.

Why, oh why, Alex wondered, as Lady Soutar fixed her with a penetrating stare, was there never an important message she needed to take, or a phone call she had to make, on occasions like this?

'Bunty,' she began awkwardly, 'I know you mean well but—'

'This isn't any of my business? Of course it isn't!' Lady Soutar exclaimed. 'But I like you—I like you a lot—and Dr Scott's a decent chap, rock solid financially, and not prone to whims or outlandish fancies. He might need a bit of tidying up in the hair department, but he's good husband material.'

'Bunty…'

'I'm sure Cumbria is a beautiful place, but there's nothing there but mountains, water and sheep.'

'Pretty much like here, really.' Alex couldn't help but laugh.

'Yes, but Kilbreckan has other attractions, wouldn't you say?' Lady Soutar said, and, despite all of her best efforts, Alex felt her cheeks heat up.

'I think every town and village has its own particular charm,' she managed to reply, and Lady Soutar sighed.

'I suppose you know what you're doing, my dear, but…I hear the police are no further forward in their attempts to recover your bike?' she continued, and, when Alex shook her head, Lady Soutar's lips thinned into a tight, white line. 'Horsewhipping. That's what these young hooligans need. A good horsewhipping.'

Alex didn't know about the horsewhipping but, with the insurance people saying they would only pay out half of what the bike had been worth because she hadn't locked it, she knew it would be years before she would be able to afford another Ducati.

'I must go, my dear,' Lady Soutar declared, 'but could you tell Dr Scott his pills seem to be doing the trick, and don't forget, if you should ever want to come back here for a holiday, my door will always be open.'

'I'll remember that,' said Alex, but she wouldn't, and Bunty Soutar knew she wouldn't.

Once she'd left Kilbreckan she would never return. There were too many memories here, too many things she wanted to forget.

Not things, her heart whispered, *people*.

People like Jamie Allen and his mother. People like Donna Ferguson, Ellie Dickson, Lady Soutar and….Hugh.

She was never going to forget Hugh, but it was better that

she left now before they both got hurt, and if her heart was already hurting it would get better in time. Everything got better, in time.

'Walk with me to my car, dear.' Lady Soutar ordered as she got stiffly to her feet. 'These old bones of mine don't like this cold weather.'

'Well, I suppose, when you're sixty, you have to expect the odd ache and pain.' Alex grinned as she accompanied Lady Soutar out into the corridor and Bunty let out a loud guffaw.

'I shall miss you, dear, but at least I'll see you one more time at the party in the village hall on Saturday night.'

'The party?' Alex repeated in confusion, then heard the phone in her room ringing. 'I'm sorry, Bunty, but I have to…'

'Answer it, dear, answer it,' Lady Soutar said, seeing Hugh emerging from his room. 'Dr Scott will help me, won't you Dr Scott?'

'I'll certainly try,' he replied, as Alex hurried back into her room. 'What's the problem?'

'No problem. I just need a strong right arm to help me out to my car,' she said but, when he took her arm, she shook her head at him. 'I hope you've got some plan up your sleeve to keep dear Alex with us. You've only got three days left, you know.'

'I know.'

'Get your hair cut first, that's my advice, then make her an offer she can't refuse,' Lady Soutar declared, fixing him with a gimlet glare. 'And I think you know what I mean by making her an offer she can't refuse.'

Hugh did, as he helped Lady Soutar into her car, and he wondered what the old lady would say if he told her his plan. Probably have him certified, he thought with an inward chuckle, although he wouldn't bet on it because Lady Soutar never failed to surprise him.

Malcolm, on the other hand, very rarely surprised him, he

thought wryly as he saw his partner tiptoeing down the corridor, looking for all the world like a bad imitation of a CIA agent.

'The ceilidh band is booked for Saturday night,' Malcolm whispered when he drew level with him. 'Jock Wilson is under strict instructions to make sure Rory Murray doesn't get up and sing, and the hall committee are on top of the catering. Is the you-know-what on its way?'

'It arrived yesterday,' Hugh murmured, 'and could you straighten up, Malcolm? If Alex sees you creeping around the corridor like that, she'll think you've got a hernia.'

'I'm trying to keep this hush-hush,' Malcolm protested. 'I thought you wanted the you-know-what to be a surprise?'

'It'll stay more of a surprise if you don't make it quite so obvious that we're hiding something,' Hugh said with exasperation.

'Oh. Right. Sorry.' Malcolm glanced over his shoulder, then back to Hugh. 'Hugh, I don't want to interfere—'

'Which means you're going to.' Hugh sighed.

'But Chrissie and I were wondering whether you were going to—you know—make one more attempt to persuade Alex to stay?'

'All I'm prepared to say, Malcolm, is that this isn't over until the fat lady sings.'

'Until the fat…' Malcolm looked confused for a second, then enlightenment spread across his face. 'You have a plan?'

Hugh nodded. 'I have a plan.'

'A good one?'

'It had better be,' Hugh said wryly, 'because it's the only one I've got.'

'I think that just about wraps up this morning's debriefing,' Hugh declared as he sat back in his seat, and Alex and Malcolm closed their notebooks, 'other than I'm pleased to report that Donna Ferguson's fingers are almost back to normal, her stomach pains have gone, and she said to me this morning that she has twice the energy she had ten years ago.'

'I'm so pleased for her,' Alex said. 'Are the test results back yet for her daughters?'

'They came this morning,' Hugh replied. 'Fiona definitely has haemochromatosis, and Morag doesn't. I've asked Chrissie to send a letter to Fiona asking her to come in so we can start treating her.'

'Speaking of letters,' Malcolm observed. 'Will the advertisement for the part-time receptionist's job be in the newspaper this week?'

'What advertisement?' Alex said, glancing across at him, but it was Hugh who replied.

'Chrissie's been working flat out for far too long. She doesn't want to give up the work completely, so Malcolm and I have decided to employ another receptionist and she and Chrissie will share the workload.'

Malcolm and he had decided, Alex thought. Without telling her. Well, of course, they hadn't told her. She was leaving in three days. She was temporary, just passing through, and any changes they made to the practice had nothing to do with her except, stupidly, illogically, she felt hurt, excluded, sidelined.

'Bunty Soutar said something odd this morning,' she declared, deliberately changing the subject. 'She said she would see me at the party in the village hall on Saturday. What party?'

Hugh swore under his breath and Malcolm looked distinctly annoyed.

'It was supposed to be a secret,' Malcolm protested. 'The villagers have arranged a farewell party for you. It's nothing fancy, just a few sandwiches, maybe some sausage rolls—'

'I wish they hadn't,' Alex interrupted. 'I mean, it's very kind of them,' she added quickly, seeing Hugh's face grow tight, 'but I really don't want a lot of fuss.'

'Can't you let go of your "I want to be alone" stance for just one evening when everyone's put so much effort into the occasion?' Hugh exclaimed, and Alex reddened.

'I didn't mean I won't go,' she replied. 'I just meant—things like that—occasions like that—I find them a bit embarrassing.'

'Because people care enough about you—like you enough—to want to throw a party for you?' Hugh shook his head. 'Maybe you need to examine your values, Alex.'

'And maybe I just don't like being pushed into the spot-light,' Alex snapped. 'Ever thought about that?'

Hugh opened his mouth, then closed it again, and Malcolm got to his feet, shaking his head as he did so.

'If there's nothing else, I'm off out on the home visits, and if this is a sample of your plan, Hugh, we're dead ducks.'

'What plan?' Alex said when Malcolm had gone.

Hugh picked up the pen from his desk and turned it round in his fingers, his expression unreadable.

'Private joke,' he said.

'Right.' Alex nodded. 'I see.'

She didn't see. All she knew was that, ever since she'd told him she wasn't staying on in Kilbreckan, post-surgery meet-ings had become excruciating. She knew he was hurting—she was hurting, too—but, if they weren't circling one another awkwardly, he was sniping at her, and this wasn't how she wanted it to end.

'Hugh…' She stared at him helplessly. 'I'll be gone in three days. Can't we at least—?'

'Shake hands, part as friends, wish each other a nice life?' he finished for her. 'No, we can't, or at least I sure as hell can't. You know what I want, Alex.'

'Hugh—'

'Sorry to interrupt you, Doctors,' Chrissie said as she stuck her head round Hugh's door, 'but Grace Allen is here with Jamie. She knows surgery is over for the morning, but she wonders if one of you could take a look at Jamie's stitches, see if they're ready to come out yet. She would have been here earlier, but with Ewan being back home now, and still not able to do much for himself…'

'Send her along, Chrissie,' Hugh replied. 'Alex and I will both take a look at Jamie's stitches.'

It was the last thing Alex wanted, but she could hardly say so.

'Let's hope Jamie's stitches are ready to come out today,' she said instead when Chrissie had disappeared. 'They weren't ready last week.'

'No,' Hugh replied.

He looked tired, she thought, sneaking a glance at him, as though he hadn't been sleeping well recently.

She hadn't been sleeping well, either, without him.

Don't go that way, Alex, her mind warned as his eyes met hers, and she was the one who looked away first. *Don't go that way. Three days. You only have to get through the next three days, and then you'll never see Hugh Scott again.*

A thought that was so overwhelmingly depressing that she positively beamed when Hugh's consulting room opened and Jamie and his mother trooped in.

'I hope these stitches are ready to come out,' Jamie declared irritably as his mother lifted him on to Hugh's examination table. 'They're dead itchy.'

Which was a good sign, and one look at Jamie's forehead was enough to tell Alex the stitches were ready to be removed.

'Do you want to do the honours, or shall I?' she said, glancing across at Hugh.

'You, I think,' he said, and Alex pulled on a pair of surgical gloves, and reached for her forceps.

The sutures didn't take long to remove, and when Alex had taken out the last one, she sat back on her heels with satisfaction.

'Now that,' she said, 'is looking really, *really* good.'

'Should it still be quite so pink?' Grace said uncertainly as she stared at her son's forehead.

'Pink is good,' Alex replied. 'Pink means it's healing, and there's no puckering or tightening of the skin at all which means in a few months' time you'll hardly be able to see that Jamie had such a bad wound. You did a superb job, Hugh.'

'I wanted to be left with a big scar,' Jamie complained. 'I wanted to look like what'shisname, the boy wizard in all the books.'

'He has a zigzag scar, Jamie,' Grace Allen observed.

'Does not,' Jamie retorted, and his mother wearily pushed her hair back from her face.

'If you say so,' she said.

'You're looking a bit stressed today, Grace,' Hugh declared, and Mrs Allen managed a smile.

'I'm a little bit tired, to be honest, Doctor. Ewan's not proving to be the most patient of patients, and my back's been giving me a bit of trouble these last two days.'

'Get Ewan's brothers to help you,' Hugh ordered. 'Most of them are plenty old enough to help carry some of the load.'

'I'll do that, Doctor,' Grace Allen replied, wincing slightly as she lifted Jamie back off the examination table, 'and I'll also try to keep this wee pest out of your surgery for a while, but I'm afraid I can't guarantee it.'

'She's doing too much,' Alex observed after Mrs Allen and Jamie had left. 'She needs to ease off a little, or she's going to be ill herself.'

'I'm afraid Grace's interpretation of the words, "ease off" would be to take a five-minute break,' Hugh said wryly, 'but I'll have a word with her husband, see if he can lean on their sons to get them to pull their weight more.'

'And I really must get on with my paperwork,' Alex exclaimed, rising to her feet.

'But you'll be coming to the party on Saturday night?' Hugh pressed, and Alex nodded.

'You know I will,' she said. 'No matter what you might think of me, I won't disappoint the villagers.'

'You couldn't disappoint anyone, *leannan*,' Hugh said softly. 'You might infuriate them, drive them crazy sometimes, but you'd never disappoint.'

'I…' She swallowed, hard. 'I'll take that as a compliment.'

'It was meant as one,' he said, his quicksilver eyes gentle. 'Alex—'

He didn't get a chance to say any more. His consulting room suddenly banged open, and Chrissie was standing there, white-faced, and trembling.

'It's…it's Grace,' she stammered. 'She stopped at my desk to have a word with me on her way out, and she was talking, telling me about Ewan, and then…Hugh, she just went down like a stone.'

'Get Jamie out of the waiting room, Chrissie,' Hugh ordered as he grabbed the defibrillator. 'Put him anywhere but get him out of sight of his mother, then dial 999. Alex, bring an ambu-bag.'

He had gone before either woman could reply and, as Chrissie hurried off to get Jamie and phone for an ambulance, Alex grabbed an ambu-bag from Hugh's store cupboard, then raced down the corridor to the waiting room to find him kneeling beside Grace, and to her horror he was administering CPR.

'I've no pulse, and she's not breathing,' he said, his voice tight.

SCA, Alex thought, as she slipped the oxygen mask over Grace's face and began squeezing the bag as hard as she could. It couldn't be anything but sudden cardiac arrest, but it didn't seem possible, credible. Grace had been laughing and joking at the exercise class just yesterday, fooling around to keep everybody motivated, and now she was lying on the floor, her lips blue and her face deathly white.

'Where's Jamie?' she asked.

'Chrissie's got him in her office, playing on her computer,' Hugh replied. 'I don't know how long it will keep him occupied—we've no games on it—but I didn't want him in here, seeing this.'

Alex didn't want to be seeing it either, couldn't believe it was happening when, only a few minutes ago, she and Hugh had been arguing about the party.

'You'd better take off her jewellery so I can shock her.'

Alex nodded and kept on squeezing the ambu-bag while she slipped off Grace's rings because, without oxygen, Grace's brain would die.

Quickly, Hugh placed one of the pads connected to the portable defibrillator on the upper right side of Grace's chest, and then affixed the other pad to her lower left side.

'Ready?' he said, and Alex nodded, and leant back, so she wouldn't come into contact with either Grace or the leads from the machine.

Hugh hit the orange button to deliver a shock, and Grace convulsed slightly but, when Alex stared at the LCD screen, there was nothing but a straight flat line.

'Come on, Grace, *come on*,' Hugh muttered, his face drawn. 'Who's going to keep your boys in line if you're not here to do it. I'm going to shock her again, Alex, so keep clear.'

She did as he said, and he hit the orange button again, but still the monitor line remained stubbornly flat.

'Any pulse at all?' he asked, and she shook her head.

Faintly she could hear Jamie talking excitedly to Chrissie about something he had seen on her computer screen, and desperately she prayed that he would stay in the receptionist's office because they were running out of time. When a patient suffered a massive cardiac arrest, there was only a small window of opportunity to bring them back, and that window was closing, fast.

'*Come on*, Grace!' Hugh exclaimed as he hit the orange button, again, and again. 'Breathe, damn you, *breathe.*'

Still nothing happened, and then Alex saw the flat line on the monitor jump slightly, begin to move erratically up and down, and then wonderfully—miraculously—it settled into a more even rhythm.

'You've got her, Hugh,' she cried, closing her eyes and sending up a silent prayer of thanks. 'She's back—she's back!'

And the paramedics were there, and within seconds they were carrying Grace out to the ambulance, and it was only when they had gone, and Chrissie had whisked Jamie away with a promise of a magazine from the newsagent's, that Alex realised she was trembling.

'Oh, God, Hugh, that was scary,' she said. 'Seriously, seriously scary.'

'Because it was real, Alex,' he replied, his eyes fixed on hers. 'Because you being here made a difference to the outcome, just as you being here has made a difference for Donna, and Jamie, and Irene Nolan, and all the other patients you've seen. It's where you're meant to be, where you were born to be.'

'Subtle you are not,' she said a little shakily, and a small smile appeared at the corner of his lips.

'Perhaps not, but I am honest. Think about it, Alex,' he said as the phone in his room began to ring, 'because you still have time to change your mind.'

And before she could reply, he had hurried off, leaving her staring after him.

On Saturday night, Alex shook her head ruefully as she gazed out over the crowded village hall. Malcolm had said the party would be 'nothing fancy', but if this was what he meant by 'nothing fancy' she couldn't begin to imagine what a 'push the boat out' party would be like.

Every man, woman and child from Kilbreckan and the surrounding area seemed to be there, the tables were groaning with food, a ceilidh band was playing a rousing medley of toe-tapping tunes, and across the small stage somebody had strung a banner with the words *Bon Voyage, Dr Alex*.

'Having a good time?' Malcolm shouted above the chatter and laughter, and she nodded.

'Great—absolutely great,' she said, except that Hugh had stayed as far away from her as possible all evening, which was understandable—of course it was—but that hadn't stopped her eyes from following him.

'You look lovely tonight,' Malcolm continued. 'Hugh was just saying the same thing to me a moment ago.'

But not to me, she thought. He's barely exchanged two words with me, and though she knew it was stupid to care, that it was better this way, she did care. She found she cared a lot.

'Looks like it's show time,' Malcolm observed, seeing Lady Soutar jerking her head at him and pointing imperiously at the stage. 'Ready for your big moment, Alex?'

As she'd ever be, Alex thought, as Malcolm began pushing his way through the throng, and reluctantly she followed him, knowing what was coming. Someone would say how sorry they all were she was leaving, one of the children from the village school would present her with a bouquet of flowers, and then she would be expected to make a speech, and she hated making speeches, hated being in the limelight, but there was no way she could get out of this.

Malcolm had already got up on the stage by the time she reached the front of the hall, and he waited only until she was there beside him before he called for silence.

'OK, it goes without saying that we shall all miss you, Alex,' he said, and there was a rumbled chorus of '*Damn shame*,' and '*I wish she was staying on*.' 'You've been a real asset to the practice, both personally and professionally, and we felt we could not let you go without giving you a party.'

Someone shouted, '*Get on with it, Doc*,' and Malcolm wagged his finger at the offender, and Alex stared out over the assembled throng.

So many faces she knew, so many people she'd met and liked. Lady Soutar, Ellie Dickson and her husband with little Alexandra, all of the Allens, apart from Grace who was still in hospital, Donna Ferguson, even Frank and Irene Nolan had come, and Hugh. Hugh was standing at the very back of the hall, leaning against the wall, his dark face inscrutable, and she looked away from him quickly.

'We also all know how much your bike meant to you,' Malcolm continued, 'and for it to be stolen while you were here with us… We all feel very badly about it, and feel, too, that we should try to make amends.'

'For God's sake, put the woman out of her misery, doc,' Rory Murray protested, and Malcolm grinned.

'OK, Neil. Bring it on stage.'

Bring what on stage? Alex wondered, but before she even had time to guess Neil Allen had appeared from the wings, and he was pushing a gleaming red Ducati. A Ducati that had a huge bow, and a big heart-shaped balloon with the words *Good Luck, Doc*! tied to its handlebars.

'Is this…?' Alex looked helplessly at Malcolm and then out at the villagers standing in front of her. 'Is this for me?'

Malcolm nodded. 'Every nut, bolt and cylinder head. Hugh told us about the Lisbon to Dakar rally, that there's no way you can afford to buy a replacement bike for it in time, so this is our farewell gift to you.'

'But I can't accept this,' Alex protested. 'It's too much— way too much.'

'We all put a little something in,' Malcolm said briskly, 'and Lady Soutar was most generous.'

'Would have come with you to Lisbon myself, Alex, if I'd only been five years younger,' Bunty exclaimed from the floor of the hall, and, when Malcolm's eyebrows rose slightly, she added, 'Oh, very well, make that ten years younger, and it's a measure of the great affection I feel for Alex that you'll get me to admit that.'

A ripple of laughter ran around the hall, and Alex shook her head.

'I…I don't know what to say,' she began. 'For you all to have…I'm not often speechless…'

'You can say that again.' Malcolm grinned, and everybody laughed, and Alex tried to smile but it wasn't easy when there was a hard lump in her throat.

'All I can say is thank you,' she said. 'Thank you so much, and I'll never forget this, or…' Her eyes sought for and found Hugh at the back of the hall. 'Or anybody here.'

A big cheer went up, and people were talking, and laughing, but she scarcely heard them. Her eyes were fixed on Hugh, and when his lips curved into a slight smile, and he gave her an almost imperceptible nod, her heart clenched and twisted inside her, and she suddenly realised what she should have seen a long time ago.

That he was right. That the challenges she had set herself had simply been a way of running away from what frightened her the most instead of standing and facing the fear. That she didn't want to climb any more mountains, take up any more extreme sports, or set herself any more New Year challenges. She wanted to stay right here because she had a different challenge now. A challenge that was a hundred times more scary than any other challenge she had ever faced before.

Quickly she moved to the steps leading down from the stage, but Malcolm barred her way.

'Are you pleased?' he said, his face beaming. 'About the bike?'

'Absolutely.' She nodded, trying to sidestep him.

'It was Hugh's idea,' Malcolm continued. 'He knew how much taking part in the rally meant to you, so he put it to the community council and they agreed unanimously.'

'It was kind of him—of you all,' she said, making a detour round him, but she didn't get far.

Someone said, '*Come back and tell us all about your trip, Doc*,' and someone else said, '*Be careful when you're out there, dear*,' and by the time she'd pushed her way through the throng Hugh was gone.

Well, why should he stay? she thought forlornly. She'd made her feelings plain so many times, so why would he stay?

'Alex?'

She turned to see Malcolm standing behind her, and managed a smile.

'I suppose I'd better circulate,' she said. 'Thank everyone in person.'

'Go after him, Alex.'

'It would be so rude,' she said, looking at the happy faces of the villagers. 'This evening is supposed to be for me.'

'I'll tell them you're on call,' Malcolm replied, then gave her a gentle push. 'Just *go*, Alex.'

She did. She slipped out of the hall, and walked up Kilbreckan High Street, but the closer she got to Hugh's house the slower her feet became.

It was all very well for her to decide that she wanted to stay here, but what if Hugh didn't want to hear that—what if he no longer cared?

'Oh, come on, Alex,' she muttered out loud when she came to a halt outside his house and saw the light on in his sitting room. 'You've been skydiving and white water rafting. How much more scary can this be?'

Downright terrifying, was the short answer, she thought, as she went into the house, took a deep breath, then knocked tentatively on his sitting-room door.

The door opened quickly, and Hugh looked surprised to see her.

'Surely the party hasn't finished already?' he said.

'No, it's still going on,' she replied, 'but I wanted—I felt—I should thank you for suggesting my farewell gift to the villagers—for organising it.'

He shrugged. 'No problem.'

The conversation was clearly over as far as he was concerned, but she couldn't let it be over, and she took a step forward.

'Can I come in?' she said, and when his eyebrows rose she added quickly, 'There's something I want to say. I won't stay long,' she continued as her gaze fell on the piles of papers strewn about his sitting room. 'You're clearly busy, but I want—I have—to say something.'

'OK,' he said, stepping back. 'So, what's so all-fired important that it made you leave a good party?'

She clasped her hands together tightly, and took a deep breath.

'I…I've been thinking about what you said about the challenges I set myself, how they're not real, and…' She took another deep breath. 'You were right, and if the offer of a permanent post with your practice is still open, I'd like to accept it.'

'Good,' he said, his face unreadable. 'That's good news.'

'Obviously, I'll—'

'Need time off in January to take part in the rally?' He nodded. 'Not a problem. Malcolm and I have managed on our own for quite a while so getting by without you for a couple of weeks in January won't harm us.'

'Actually, I was going to say I'll obviously need to find somewhere else to live,' she said awkwardly. 'I can't keep on living in your flat.'

'Especially not when I'm intending to reconvert it back into a single home,' he agreed. 'I'll make enquiries in the village, see if anybody has a cottage they'd be prepared to let you rent on a long lease.'

'Right,' she said. 'So…that's settled then?'

'Looks like it,' he observed.

'Good.' She nodded. 'Well, as I said, you're obviously very busy, and I…I have things to do.'

Like trying to figure out how, when I've screwed this up so badly, I can possibly make it right again, she thought.

'Actually, before you go,' he said. 'There's something I'd like to show you—get your opinion of.'

'Get my opinion of?' she repeated, and he nodded.

'It's in the garage.'

'Hugh, if you've bought yourself a new car, I'm really not the best person to ask for advice,' she said, as she followed him out of the house and round to his garage. 'I'm a biker, remember?'

'It's not a new car,' he replied, as he unlocked the garage doors. 'It's something a whole lot more spectacular.'

It was, because when he opened the garage doors, and switched on the light, her jaw dropped. There was a motorcycle sitting next to his Range Rover. A brand new Ducati 1000, but this one was blue, not red.

'You've bought a *bike*?' she gasped.

'Went down to Inverness after work last night and collected it,' he said.

'But I don't understand,' she said slowly. 'I mean, I know you said you were a biker when you were a med student, and I think it's great you've bought yourself one, but when are you ever going to ride it?'

'In the Lisbon to Dakar rally. I wired my entrance fee to the organisers this morning. I still have my hotel accommodation to sort out for the first night before the rally starts,' he continued, 'but I expect I'll get in somewhere.'

She stared at him in blank disbelief for a second, then rounded on him.

'Hugh, are you *insane*? People *die* in that race, and you haven't been on a motorbike for years.'

'Alex, it's the ultimate challenge, the opportunity of a lifetime.'

'What kind of idiot would say that?' she protested. 'It's a *stupid* thing to say.'

A smile creased his lips.

'It's what you said, when you told me you'd entered,' he pointed out, and she shook her head at him.

'But I ride every day,' she exclaimed, 'Have done for years. Even if you take your bike out every day between now and January, you'll still be a rookie. You can't do this, Hugh, you honestly *can't*—'

'Alex, if you're going to Lisbon to take part in the race, I'm coming with you,' he exclaimed. 'I won't ride beside you, get in your way, encroach on your personal space, but I need to be there, to make sure you're all right.'

'No,' she said, vehemently shaking her head. 'I won't allow you to do that. What if you get hurt, what if you…if you should die?'

'Why should you care what happens to me?' he said, his eyes dark and penetrating in the dim garage light.

'Because…because I love you, you big idiot,' she said. 'Because I wouldn't get a minute's rest, or a moment's sleep, for worrying about you.'

'And now you know how I feel,' he said softly. 'I love you, Alex Lorimer, and I want to spend the rest of my life with you. I don't know how long we'll have together. I'm hoping it's going to be years and years, until you're a little old lady, and I'm a little old man, but whatever the future brings, I want us to face it together.'

'Hugh—'

'No, please, let me finish,' he insisted. 'I know what you're going to say. That you're scared you'll hurt me by dying, but, *leannan*, don't you understand that living without you, knowing you were living somewhere else, miles away from me, would be a hundred times worse for me?'

'I don't want to be without you either,' she said softly. 'Which is why—'

'I know you think you'll somehow fail me because you can't give me children,' he interrupted, 'but, hell, Alex, I don't know whether *I* can father children. Jenny was on the Pill the whole time we were married because we didn't want to start a family right away, so for all I know I might be infertile, too, and even if I'm not, can't you see, even now, that it's *you* I want? Only you. Nobody but you.'

She reached up and touched his cheek, her throat so tight she could hardly speak.

'Can I say something now?' she said.

'Will I want to hear it?' he replied, his expression uncertain, unsure, and she managed a tremulous smile.

'Hugh, I don't want to climb any more mountains, or take part in any more extreme sports. I don't even want to take part in the rally. You asked me something—it seems a lifetime ago now—and you said you would make it your lifetime aim to persuade me to say it without qualification.'

'I remember.' He nodded.

'Ask me again, Hugh.'

He searched her face, then reached out and clasped her hands in his, and she heard him take a deep breath.

'Alex, do you trust me?' he said, and her smile widened.

'Yes,' she said simply. 'Yes, I trust you.'

'You do?' he said, and his face lit up with so much love, that if Alex hadn't already been in love with him that would have done it. 'And you'll marry me?'

'Yes, I'll marry you,' she whispered. 'Hugh, I'd marry you right this minute if I could.'

And he drew her into his arms, and kissed her, and when she surfaced, breathlessly, clutching onto his shirt, she knew she had no doubts, no misgivings, that he had taken them all away.

All except one, she realised, as her gaze fell on his blue Ducati motorbike.

'Hugh, what are we going to do about the bike the villagers bought me?' she said uncertainly. 'They only bought it because they thought I was going to enter the rally. I'll have to give it back.'

'No, you won't. Not if you actually go to Portugal,' he replied.

'But, I don't want to take part in—'

'Not to take part in the rally,' he said, 'but for our honeymoon.'

'Our honeymoon?' she repeated. 'In January?'

'I don't want to wait a second longer than I have to,' he said, gathering her back into his arms.

She didn't either.

'There's just three things I want you to promise me, Hugh,' she said into his chest, 'and then I'll definitely marry you in January.'

'Anything you want,' he murmured huskily.

'I may be a sporty girl, but I'm not sleeping in a tent on our honeymoon. I want to stay in a proper hotel, with a big double bed, and a bath and a toilet.'

'Wuss,' he said, kissing the top of her head. 'And the second thing?'

'I want you to wear a kilt at our wedding, so I can see just how bony your knees really are before I say "*I do*."'

He tilted her chin and gave her a hard stare. 'You drive a very hard bargain, Alex Lorimer, but, yes, I'll wear a kilt. And the third thing?'

She stretched up, and touched his hair.

'Maybe Bunty's right. Maybe you *should* get your hair cut.'

And he laughed, and kissed her again.

0108 Gen Std HB

MILLS & BOON®
Pure reading pleasure

FEBRUARY 2008 HARDBACK TITLES

ROMANCE

The Italian Billionaire's Pregnant Bride *Lynne Graham*	978 0 263 20238 0
The Guardian's Forbidden Mistress *Miranda Lee*	978 0 263 20239 7
Secret Baby, Convenient Wife *Kim Lawrence*	978 0 263 20240 3
Caretti's Forced Bride *Jennie Lucas*	978 0 263 20241 0
The Salvatore Marriage Deal *Natalie Rivers*	978 0 263 20242 7
The British Billionaire Affair *Susanne James*	978 0 263 20243 4
One-Night Love-Child *Anne McAllister*	978 0 263 20244 1
Virgin: Wedded at the Italian's Convenience *Diana Hamilton*	978 0 263 20245 8
The Bride's Baby *Liz Fielding*	978 0 263 20246 5
Expecting a Miracle *Jackie Braun*	978 0 263 20247 2
Wedding Bells at Wandering Creek *Patricia Thayer*	978 0 263 20248 9
The Loner's Guarded Heart *Michelle Douglas*	978 0 263 20249 6
Sweetheart Lost and Found *Shirley Jump*	978 0 263 20250 2
The Single Dad's Patchwork Family *Claire Baxter*	978 0 263 20251 9
His Island Bride *Marion Lennox*	978 0 263 20252 6
Desert Prince, Expectant Mother *Olivia Gates*	978 0 263 20253 3

HISTORICAL

Lady Gwendolen Investigates *Anne Ashley*	978 0 263 20189 5
The Unknown Heir *Anne Herries*	978 0 263 20190 1
Forbidden Lord *Helen Dickson*	978 0 263 20191 8

MEDICAL™

The Doctor's Royal Love-Child *Kate Hardy*	978 0 263 19867 6
A Consultant Beyond Compare *Joanna Neil*	978 0 263 19871 3
The Surgeon Boss's Bride *Melanie Milburne*	978 0 263 19875 1
A Wife Worth Waiting For *Maggie Kingsley*	978 0 263 19879 9

0108 Gen Std LP

Pure reading pleasure

FEBRUARY 2008 LARGE PRINT TITLES

ROMANCE

The Greek Tycoon's Virgin Wife *Helen Bianchin*	978 0 263 20018 8
Italian Boss, Housekeeper Bride	978 0 263 20019 5
Sharon Kendrick	
Virgin Bought and Paid For *Robyn Donald*	978 0 263 20020 1
The Italian Billionaire's Secret Love-Child	978 0 263 20021 8
Cathy Williams	
The Mediterranean Rebel's Bride *Lucy Gordon*	978 0 263 20022 5
Found: Her Long-Lost Husband *Jackie Braun*	978 0 263 20023 2
The Duke's Baby *Rebecca Winters*	978 0 263 20024 9
Millionaire to the Rescue *Ally Blake*	978 0 263 20025 6

HISTORICAL

Masquerading Mistress *Sophia James*	978 0 263 20121 5
Married By Christmas *Anne Herries*	978 0 263 20125 3
Taken By the Viking *Michelle Styles*	978 0 263 20129 1

MEDICAL™

The Italian GP's Bride *Kate Hardy*	978 0 263 19932 1
The Consultant's Italian Knight	978 0 263 19933 8
Maggie Kingsley	
Her Man of Honour *Melanie Milburne*	978 0 263 19934 5
One Special Night... *Margaret McDonagh*	978 0 263 19935 2
The Doctor's Pregnancy Secret *Leah Martyn*	978 0 263 19936 9
Bride for a Single Dad *Laura Iding*	978 0 263 19937 6

0208 Gen Std HB

MILLS & BOON
Pure reading pleasure

MARCH 2008 HARDBACK TITLES

ROMANCE

The Markonos Bride *Michelle Reid*	978 0 263 20254 0
The Italian's Passionate Revenge *Lucy Gordon*	978 0 263 20255 7
The Greek Tycoon's Baby Bargain *Sharon Kendrick*	978 0 263 20256 4
Di Cesare's Pregnant Mistress *Chantelle Shaw*	978 0 263 20257 1
The Billionaire's Virgin Mistress *Sandra Field*	978 0 263 20258 8
At the Sicilian Count's Command *Carole Mortimer*	978 0 263 20259 5
Blackmailed For Her Baby *Elizabeth Power*	978 0 263 20260 1
The Cattle Baron's Virgin Wife *Lindsay Armstrong*	978 0 263 20261 8
His Pregnant Housekeeper *Caroline Anderson*	978 0 263 20262 5
The Italian Playboy's Secret Son *Rebecca Winters*	978 0 263 20263 2
Her Sheikh Boss *Carol Grace*	978 0 263 20264 9
Wanted: White Wedding *Natasha Oakley*	978 0 263 20265 6
The Heir's Convenient Wife *Myrna Mackenzie*	978 0 263 20266 3
Coming Home to the Cattleman *Judy Christenberry*	978 0 263 20267 0
Billionaire Doctor, Ordinary Nurse *Carol Marinelli*	978 0 263 20268 7
The Sheikh Surgeon's Baby *Meredith Webber*	978 0 263 20269 4

HISTORICAL

The Last Rake In London *Nicola Cornick*	978 0 263 20192 5
The Outrageous Lady Felsham *Louise Allen*	978 0 263 20193 2
An Unconventional Miss *Dorothy Elbury*	978 0 263 20194 9

MEDICAL™

Nurse Bride, Bayside Wedding *Gill Sanderson*	978 0 263 19883 6
The Outback Doctor's Surprise Bride *Amy Andrews*	978 0 263 19887 4
A Wedding at Limestone Coast *Lucy Clark*	978 0 263 19888 1
The Doctor's Meant-To-Be Marriage *Janice Lynn*	978 0 263 19889 8

 0208 Gen Std LP

Pure reading pleasure

MARCH 2008 LARGE PRINT TITLES

ROMANCE

The Billionaire's Captive Bride *Emma Darcy*	978 0 263 20026 3
Bedded, or Wedded? *Julia James*	978 0 263 20027 0
The Boss's Christmas Baby *Trish Morey*	978 0 263 20028 7
The Greek Tycoon's Unwilling Wife *Kate Walker*	978 0 263 20029 4
Winter Roses *Diana Palmer*	978 0 263 20030 0
The Cowboy's Christmas Proposal	978 0 263 20031 7
Judy Christenberry	
Appointment at the Altar *Jessica Hart*	978 0 263 20032 4
Caring for His Baby *Caroline Anderson*	978 0 263 20033 1

HISTORICAL

Scandalous Lord, Rebellious Miss *Deb Marlowe*	978 0 263 20133 8
The Duke's Gamble *Miranda Jarrett*	978 0 263 20137 6
The Damsel's Defiance *Meriel Fuller*	978 0 263 20141 3

MEDICAL™

The Single Dad's Marriage Wish *Carol Marinelli*	978 0 263 19938 3
The Playboy Doctor's Proposal *Alison Roberts*	978 0 263 19939 0
The Consultant's Surprise Child *Joanna Neil*	978 0 263 19940 6
Dr Ferrero's Baby Secret *Jennifer Taylor*	978 0 263 19941 3
Their Very Special Child *Dianne Drake*	978 0 263 19942 0
The Surgeon's Runaway Bride *Olivia Gates*	978 0 263 19943 7

WITHDRAWN FROM STOCK